the earth-two adventures vol. 1

the vortex•the voyage•the village

John K. LaShell

i

DEDICATION

To the children of Grace Community Church
for whom these stories were written.

Those children (now grown) may note that I have changed
Siegfried's name to Hagen. Hagen is a more appropriate name
for my character because in an old German myth, Siegfried was
a hero, and Hagen was evil.

CONTENTS

PREFACE

I wrote this series of adventures in the years 1999 and 2000 while I was teaching the first through sixth graders on Wednesday evenings. At that time, our group of children all regularly attended Sunday School where they received a solid background in Bible. Not wanting to duplicate their Sunday School instruction, I used these stories to paint a picture of the kind of young people I wanted them to become. The children in these stories learn to depend on God's word as they face increasingly difficult and dangerous challenges.

Those children from my Wednesday night group are now young adults, and over the years, they have continued to encourage me to publish these stories. Now, at last, I have an opportunity to do so. Six more stories followed the three in this volume, and I hope to make them available as well.

All over the world, people seek to control the world around them with magical words. At one level, this is a deluded attempt to imitate the power of God's creative words. On the other hand, where there is smoke there is sometimes fire. Perhaps behind all the folly of magic there is a vague racial remembrance of a gift God gave to Adam and Eve. Is it possible that God intended them to use the Mother of all languages to exercise dominion over the earth and its creatures? That is the idea on which these stories are based.

The Vortex

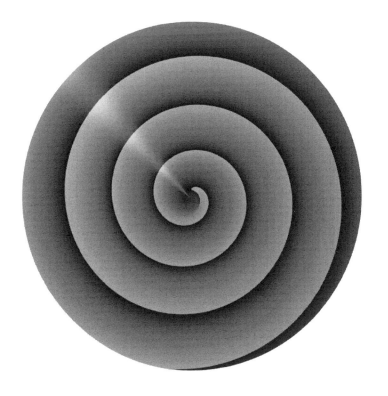

CHAPTER 1—FRIENDS

"Mom, what if the neighbor kids at our new house don't like me? I won't have anybody to play with." Harold Wilson loosened his seat belt, tucked his left ankle under the other leg and scooted around to face his mother.

Mrs. Wilson took one hand off the steering wheel to stroke her son's head. "Your dad and I think you will get along just fine. We really liked Susan and William."

Harold sighed, "I know, Mom, but William's only nine. That makes him two whole years younger than me. Susan's ten, but she's a girl. I wish William was ten instead of Susan." He studied his mother's face for a few moments. She seemed calm and cheerful, so maybe everything would be all right. He turned back to watch the road.

"Are we there yet?"

"About five minutes. We just passed the Myers' farm. They're our next closest neighbors."

The Wilsons' minivan turned the last corner right on schedule. Harold knew they had arrived because his dad's Subaru was parked on the road in front of the house, and a large yellow moving van filled the driveway. His new home and the house to the right of it were both three stories high, with walls built of rough fieldstone.

As the minivan rolled to a stop, a girl and a boy raced across the lawn from the house next door. By the time Harold unbuckled his seat belt and opened the door, they were waiting for him at the side of the road. He slid out and shut the door behind him. The boy was bouncing up and down on his toes with excitement. His sister stood quietly beside him. Her long, light brown hair moved gently in the breeze as she carefully looked Harold over. `Harold, who was normally awkward around strangers, felt even more uncomfortable than usual. The girl was pretty, and that made it worse. *I wish she'd stop staring at me,* he thought. The inspection seemed to go on forever, but it probably lasted no more than four or five seconds. Finally, the girl smiled and spoke.

"Hi. You must be Harold. I'm Susan, and this is William. Your dad said we could take you into the house to see your bedroom, but then we all have to go outside. He doesn't want us to get in the way of the movers."

Harold's dresser and bed had been set up in a large room on the second floor, but the closet was empty because the rest of his things were still in boxes on the truck. He wanted to help the movers, but his dad said no, so the three children went out to play.

"Come on," said William. "We've got a bunch of stuff to show you." He led the way between the two houses to a low, circular stone wall. "This is a hand-dug well."

Harold leaned over the edge and looked. The well was four feet wide and fifteen feet deep. In the still water at the bottom he could see a patch of blue sky and the outlines of three heads.

"Neat, huh?" said William. He dropped a small stone into the center of the circle, and they watched the ripples move out to the edge. "The water for our houses comes from another well, but my dad says this is good enough to drink."

Next, the children climbed the hill behind their houses to poke around in the crumbling ruins of an abandoned farmhouse. "This is as far as we can go," said Susan when the farmhouse had grown boring. "We have to stay in sight of our house, and there are too many trees in the way if we climb any higher."

"Last year, I found a really old penny in the dirt beside the door," added William. "I'll show it to you when we go back down. My mom found an Indian arrowhead in the field over there. Maybe if we look, we can find something else."

They searched through the ruins and the field for half an hour, but found nothing of interest. Then Mrs. Struthers called them down for sandwiches and a Coke. After lunch, Susan and William took Harold up into their tree house and swore him in as the third member of the Ends of the Earth Explorers Club.

"Why do you call it that?" asked Harold.

"We couldn't tell you before you were a member," said William. "The name comes from a verse we learned in Sunday school. You have to learn it too. It's Isaiah 45:22, 'Turn to Me and be saved, all the ends of the earth; For I am God, and there is no other.' We want to go to the ends of the earth to tell people about Jesus."

"Sometimes," said Susan, "we pick a country from the map on the kitchen wall and pretend we're missionaries there, or sometimes we act out the lives of the famous missionaries in these stories." She pointed to a small row of tattered paperback books lined up on a narrow shelf. "Do you have a favorite missionary, maybe somebody you've met or somebody you've read about?"

"No," replied Harold. "I think one came to our church once, but I was sick that day. I don't know what he does."

"We had some missionaries from Africa stay at our house overnight last year," said Susan. "Our parents let us stay up late to listen to their stories."

"Yes!" laughed William. "One morning while the man was shaving in the bathroom, he looked in the mirror and saw a cobra rising up out of the toilet behind him. It came through the pipes that led out into the jungle behind their house."

"Well, I don't think we are going to act out that story," said Susan, "not unless you want to be the cobra! My favorite missionary is Amy Carmichael who rescued girls in India, but her story doesn't have many parts for boys."

"Let's do Dr. David Livingstone," said William. "He was the first white man to explore the middle of Africa, Harold. He wanted the people there to hear about Christ. There weren't any cars or planes then, so he had to walk thousands of miles just on his feet."

"Okay," said Susan. "Harold, you can be the good Doctor."

Throughout the afternoon, Dr. Livingstone, usually known as Harold, clambered over rocks and under fallen trees to discover the largest waterfall in the world (at the small creek that ran past the Struthers' house). He freed many slaves (represented by Susan), and late in the afternoon he met the American newspaper reporter, Henry Stanley, who had been sent to find him. Stanley (played by William) looked at the only white face within thousands of miles and greeted the missionary with the now famous words, "Doctor Livingstone, I presume."

Shortly before supper, Livingstone (that is, Harold) had to kneel down in prayer and die. His two faithful African friends (Susan and William) buried his heart under a tree. "He loved Africa so much, that his heart should stay here," Susan said. "Then they carried his bones back to England, where the whole nation wept over his death."

The Wilsons ate supper with the Struthers family and then went home to unpack. On the next day, which was Sunday, the two families went to church together. And then it was Monday—Monday and school.

"Do I have to go, Mom?" Harold whined. "School will be out for the summer in just six weeks. I counted. I'll be the only new kid in the class. They'll be right in the middle of something, and I won't know what's going on. I'll look dumb."

"Yes, Harold. We've been through this all before. You have to go, so grab your backpack and get into the van."

Harold groaned and dragged himself out the door toward the driveway, but he perked up when he saw Susan and William coming across the lawn. Tomorrow he would be riding the bus with them, but today his mother was driving them all to school.

Twenty minutes later, they pulled into the school parking lot. Susan and William drifted off to visit with their friends while Harold and his mother headed to the office to fill out some papers. By the time they were finished, the starting bell had already rung, so Harold had to walk into class late. That was bad enough, but then the teacher made him stand up front and introduce himself.

Harold knew he should look at the other kids as he spoke, but he couldn't make himself do it. He looked at his feet instead. "My name is Harold Wilson," he mumbled. "We just moved into the house beside the Strutherses—you know, Susan and William? My dad had to come here for his job. Umm. I guess that's it." He sat down with his cheeks burning. *I just made a fool of myself,* he thought.

The rest of the morning passed slowly. The teacher gave Harold a chapter to read in a social studies book while the other kids worked in small groups on their semester projects. Then it was time for the noon recess. Harold hurried outside, hoping to find William or Susan, but one of the boys in his class caught up with him first.

"Hey Stupid, wait up!"

Harold stopped.

"Yes, I mean you, Bird-Brain."

The dull pain that had been gnawing at Harold's gut all morning exploded. He swallowed some horrid stuff that made its way from his stomach into the back of his throat and turned around slowly to face Lenny Richards. Harold knew the boy's name because their teacher had threatened to send him to the office for goofing off in class. Lenny was standing with his hands on his hips and a sneer on his lips.

"You better know who's in charge when the teachers aren't around, and it ain't you." Lenny crossed his arms. "I don't like your name. I think I'll call you Hairy."

Harold looked at the ground between Lenny's feet and mumbled, "Harry's not really a nickname for Harold. My mom told me Harry comes from Henry."

"I didn't say H-A-R-R-Y." Lenny laughed as he spelled out the name. "I said H-A-I-R-Y 'cause your hair would look great on a girl. My sister would love to have curls like yours. But I have a better idea; your new name is Harriet. Get it? Harold, H-A-I-R-Y, Harriet? When you hear me call 'Harriet!' you'd better come running." Lenny laughed again and shouted, "Harold's name is Harriet! Harold's name is Harriet!"

Three of the other boys began to take up the chant. "Harold's name is Harriet! Harold's name is Harriet."

Harold was standing in the center of a growing circle of children, looking down at the ground and trying not to cry when Susan burst through the ring and came to stand beside him. "Who started this?" she demanded. "Was it you, Lenny? How could you be so mean? God wants us to be kind, and that's not kind."

Most of the children became quiet and began to look uncomfortable, but not Lenny. "Shut up, preacher girl! Mind your own business!" Then he picked up the chant again: "Harold's name is Harriet! Harold's name is Harriet! Harold's name is—" Before Lenny could finish, Susan made a fist and hit him so hard on the chest that he fell to the ground. Lenny howled, "I thought you said God wants us to be kind!"

Susan didn't have a chance to answer because at that moment the playground monitor broke up the circle and hauled her and Lenny off to see the principal. As they walked away, Harold felt someone tugging at his shirtsleeve. "Come on," said

William.

William led the way to a shady spot under a tree where both boys sat down. "Harold," he said, "don't let Lenny bother you. He has his own little gang with three friends, but nobody else likes him. My dad says his whole family is as nasty as grizzly bears. They'd tear your leg off just to watch you bleed."

At the end of recess as Harold was heading back to class, he spotted Susan coming out of the office. Her head was held high, her shoulders were straight, and her lips were pressed tightly together. She never told him or William what had happened.

That evening after supper, her father took her off by herself for a long time. As William later reported, when she came back into the living room, her head was held high, her shoulders were straight, and her lips were pressed tightly together. And she never told either of the boys about that talk either.

On that day, Harold decided two things. First, when he grew up he was going to marry Susan. Second, he was going to try very hard not to make her mad.

"Mom," said Harold, as they were sitting at the supper table that evening, "do you remember a few months ago when I was complaining that I didn't have any friends?"

"Yes, Harold," said Mrs. Wilson. "I taught you a Bible verse, Proverbs 18:24. Can you still say it?"

Harold closed his eyes for a moment to gather his thoughts. Then he recited, "Proverbs 18:24, 'A man of too many friends comes to ruin, But there is a friend who sticks closer than a brother.' I've been thinking about that verse today," he said. "You told me that the first half of the verse means that people who try too hard to be popular with everybody will end up in trouble."

"That's right, Harold."

"Well, I've never been popular at all, so that part of the verse didn't fit me. But then you said that Jesus was my best friend and that He would stick closer to me than my brother, if I had one. Well, I've been wondering. Could an ordinary person stick closer to me than a brother? Could I have a second-best friend like that?"

"Yes, Harold, and I hope someday you will. Many people go through their whole lives without having that kind of a friend, but if God gives you such a friend it is a great blessing."

"One more thing, Mom. Could my second-best friend be . . . a girl?

CHAPTER 2—EXPLORERS

The six remaining weeks of school passed slowly, but there was no more trouble with Lenny. It was the first day of summer vacation, and the boys were fishing for crawdads in the creek, using bits of raw chicken liver tied to pieces of string.

Susan was sitting on a large flat rock with her knees tucked up under her chin, watching them. *Harold's mom is right*, she thought. Two days earlier, she had overheard Mrs. Wilson saying to her parents, "Harold is changing. He's not as timid as he used to be. I think your two kids have been good for him." Susan smiled to herself. She liked Harold, and it was nice to have someone new to play with her and William.

"I've got one! I've got one!" shouted William.

"Pull it up slowly," said Harold, "or it will let go. Try to grab it before you lift it out of the water."

William nodded, but when he reached for the crawdad, the small creature let go of the chicken liver and latched onto William's finger with its sharp pincers. "Ouch! Ouch! Ouch!" he cried. He shook his hand, and the crawdad fell back into the creek.

Susan and Harold both laughed.

"You wouldn't laugh if it was your finger," growled William.

Harold pulled his string out of the water. "I suppose so," he said, "but you were pretty funny." He and William went over to sit beside Susan.

"I've been thinking," said Harold. "If our club is the Ends of the Earth Explorers Club we ought to do some real exploring, and not just in our own backyards."

"Maybe we can talk our parents into letting us go alone to the vortex," said William. "Our dad took Susan and me up there last summer."

"What's a vortex," asked Harold, "and where is it?"

"It's a small, bare mound in the woods about a mile-and-a-half up the hill from here. It's in the box canyon where our creek starts," replied Susan. "Strange things happen there. When you're near enough, the needle of your compass is drawn toward the hill. It doesn't matter where you stand. The compass always points toward the hill instead of pointing north. My dad says there must be a big chunk of iron ore under the ground, or maybe a meteorite with a lot of iron in it. Some older people, who have lived here for a long time, tell scary stories about the vortex. They say it's a magical place where people can mysteriously disappear, but my dad says those are just a bunch of superstitious, old-wives' tales."

"Well, I think our Explorers Club should go to see it," said Harold. "Besides, maybe a tribe of Indians that has been hiding for a hundred years has sneaked into the canyon. We could discover them and be real missionaries and tell them about Jesus."

That night the children went to work at getting their parents' permission to go. Harold told his mom and dad that Susan and William had already been up to the end of the canyon with their father, so they knew the way. He didn't say anything about the vortex because he was afraid that his father would want to go with them to see it.

At the same time in the house next door, the Struthers children were insisting that they were much older and much more responsible than last summer when they were just little kids. Besides, there would be three of them, and Harold was nearly twelve.

After the children went to bed, the two sets of parents talked on the telephone. Susan, who was supposed to be asleep, heard her dad telling Mr. Wilson about the vortex. Then she heard her mom reassuring Mrs. Wilson that the children would not be eaten by bears. The black bears in their woods were not fierce like the Rocky Mountain grizzlies. These bears ran away whenever they saw a human being.

The next morning, three happy members of the Ends of the Earth Explorers Club began preparing for their big adventure. They put lunches, compasses, and bottles of water into their school backpacks. Susan took a small notebook to make a proper, official record of their exploration. Harold packed a small New Testament, just in case they really did meet a lost tribe of Indians. William carried a flashlight he had won at Sunday school for memorizing Bible verses. On the barrel of the flashlight were the words, "The light of the world is Jesus."

"Now remember," said Mrs. Struthers, as she gave them their final instructions, "stay close to the stream all the way up and back so you don't get lost. If you see any bears, make sure you don't get between a mother and her cub. Be back in time for supper."

"Okay," they all answered. And then they were off.

The trip up the canyon was uneventful. The children walked slowly, splashing water at each other and throwing stones into the creek, so it was nearly noon by the time they reached the vortex. They walked around it several times just to watch the effect it had on their compasses. Then they sat down on top of the mound and ate their lunches. The air was calm and warm, so Susan and Harold lay back on the grass beside the vortex to watch puffy white clouds float slowly across the face of the sky.

Susan began to dream about being a missionary in a strange land. Maybe she and William and Harold would go to preach to cannibals. When the cannibals captured her and planned to eat her for supper, Harold would volunteer to take her place, and they would let her go. She would cry and refuse to leave him. She could almost feel the flames of the cooking fire. She could almost . . .

"Susan, Harold!" William's voice was a whisper, but it was a loud, frightened whisper. "This place is creepy. Watch." William pulled a pink petal from a stem of wild roses he held in his hand. He dropped it, and the petal floated slowly over to the center of the mound to join a small pile of similar petals.

"That's nothing," said Susan. "There must be a breeze that's too light for you to feel. The breeze is blowing the petals into a pile."

William said nothing. He moved to the opposite side of the mound and repeated the experiment. The petal floated down to join the others. "It doesn't matter where I stand," he whispered. "They all land in the same spot. Like I said, this place is creepy."

"I agree, William," said Harold. "That is weird. Rose petals aren't magnetic. There must be something else drawing them to the center of the vortex."

"We didn't see anything like that last year," said Susan. "I wonder why?"

"Well, you probably didn't try William's experiment," Harold replied. "Plus, if there was any wind at all, the experiment wouldn't work. The wind would just scatter the petals before they reached the ground." He paused for a moment then added, "Do you think this is a door into another world? Maybe Narnia is a real place after all. If we could think of the right magic word, maybe the door would open!"

Susan was about to say, "That's silly," but Harold looked serious, so she bit her lip and said, "I suppose it wouldn't hurt to try. After all, even if it is a magic door, we're not liable to find the right words to open it."

They tried all the magic words they could remember— abracadabra, hocus pocus, open sesame, and even supercalifragilisticexpialidocious. Finally, William said, "Maybe it's something really simple. We want to go in, so why don't we just hold hands, close our eyes and concentrate on getting in and then say 'in' together." So they tried it.

"I felt something," said Susan after they had opened their eyes.

"So did I," said Harold. "It felt as if the ground moved just a little bit."

"Let's try it again," urged William. So they did, several times, and always with the same result. The ground seemed to quiver, but that was all.

"If this vortex has been here for a long time," said Harold, "maybe whoever made it didn't speak English, so the door won't open for an English word. Let's go back home. We won't tell anybody about it 'cause they'll just think we're making everything up, but let's find as many ways of saying 'in' as we can. Then we can come back up here and try them all out."

For the next week, the children were very busy trying to find as many different ways as they could to say "in." At church, they talked to old Mr. Schwartz. He was German, but he also knew Russian and Italian. Susan's piano teacher was Korean, so she asked her. When Harold and his parents went to lunch at a Chinese restaurant, Harold asked to speak to the cook. A trip to the library yielded several more words. By the end of the week, they had found seventeen ways of saying "in" or "into." Susan worked them all into a rhyming chant, which the children memorized before their next hike to the vortex.

The day was warm, the sky was clear, and the air was calm as the children stood nervously at the top of the vortex mound. They held hands, closed their eyes and recited their chant together. This time the ground did not simply quiver. It shook violently and then began to spin slowly. The children clung tightly to each other with their eyes closed until the spinning stopped. Harold's eyes remained closed until they were jerked open by the sound of Susan screaming.

CHAPTER 3—MAGIC?

Susan and William stood with their mouths and their eyes wide open, staring at something behind Harold. Harold let go of their hands, spun around, and shoved the younger children behind him. Three or four feet in front of him stood a man.

He was taller than Harold's father, who was just over six feet. He wore a forest-green shirt and pants, high leather boots, and a hooded cape that shifted from brown to gray to green as it fluttered in the breeze. A large knife at his waist, a small pack on his back, and a long, gnarled walking stick completed his outfit.

It was the face of the stranger, however, that captured Harold's attention. It was the face of an old man, without the usual wrinkles or the gray hair. It was the face of a dangerous man, who also could be kind. It was the face of a man who could look into your eyes and see if you were telling the truth or not. Right now that face was stern, and the stranger's eyes were fixed on Harold.

"Who—who—who are you," stammered Harold, "and where are we?"

"I could, with equal justice, ask who you are," replied the stranger. "You may call me Ulysses, the wanderer. As for your second question, you are no longer in your world. But come. Sit down. It takes a great deal of energy to open the door, so you are, no doubt, hungry and tired. If you brought anything to eat, this would be a good time for a snack. You have quite a walk ahead of you before I can send you back home."

The children sat down obediently and began to eat the granola bars they had brought for an afternoon snack . They felt as tired as if they had just climbed a high mountain or spent the whole day digging in the garden. As they ate, the children looked around. They were sitting in a box canyon next to a mound that looked like their vortex. A small stream, much like their stream, came out of the base of a cliff at the end of the canyon, but the trees around them were larger than the trees in their familiar woods, and the day had suddenly turned cloudy.

"Now," said Ulysses, "tell me who you are, how you managed to open the door, and why you have come."

Susan told their story, with frequent interruptions from William and Harold. When she had finished, she added, "We didn't really expect anything to happen. It was just a game." She paused for a moment and then added, "Well, I guess we were hoping for some kind of adventure."

"Please tell us where we are," said William. "This almost looks like our canyon, but it's not quite the same, and the vortex doesn't draw the needle of my compass away from the north anymore. You said we came through a door, but a doorway to where? Are we in Narnia, or Neverland, or the Land of Oz?"

Ulysses paused for a moment and then said, "Well, I suppose it won't hurt. You are a very observant young man. Get up. We can talk as we walk." They stood, stretched, and started down the canyon. "You are not in Narnia or any other fairytale land. In fact, you are still on Earth. Or, more precisely, you are on Earth-Two."

"Earth-Two?" said Harold. "You mean there is more than one planet Earth?" He wrinkled his nose and tried to wrap his mind around the idea. "Are we in an alternate universe, like in the movies?"

"Yes to the first question," said Ulysses. "I will try to explain. When you look at a stone, it seems to be perfectly solid, but as a matter of fact, the atoms that make up the stone are separated by a lot of empty space. Now imagine that right next to each atom in the stone, you could place an exact duplicate of that atom. You would have two identical stones in the space originally occupied by one. Of course, you would need to make sure that the atoms of the second stone could not interfere with the atoms of the first stone."

Susan and Harold nodded—Susan had read a book and Harold had seen a show on TV about all the empty space in solid objects—but William just shrugged, and mumbled, "I don't get it."

Apparently, Ulysses didn't hear him because he kept on talking. "Thousands of years ago, God did something like that. He created Earth-Two inside, or beside, the original Earth, your Earth. At first they were identical, but in time certain changes occurred. Your Earth, for example, has large cities in places where we don't even have villages. The tall trees in your canyon were cut down about sixty years ago; these have never been cut.

"So would our canyon have looked more like this one sixty years ago?" asked William.

"That's right," replied Ulysses. "For the most part the two Earths cannot touch each other, but on every continent, God has created doors between the worlds. The doors only work going in one direction. You came into our Earth by an entrance door, but you can't go out that way. I am taking you to the nearest exit door."

"How long is it going to take?" William asked.

"Two or three hours," answered Ulysses. "Then you'll have to walk home from there. I doubt you'll make it back in time for supper."

The three children, who were walking together behind Ulysses, looked at each other in dismay. "We're so in trouble," mouthed Susan.

Ulysses continued—without noticing Susan's comment. "As far as I know, you are the only people in all of history to enter a door by accident. You must never come again because without my help you might not be able to return to your world. These woods are filled with many wild and dangerous animals, and there are no towns close by. Normally no one would be around to help you, but I am here on another mission. Soon I will be finished, and then I will be gone."

"So we just guessed the magic word that opened the door? Is that what happened?" asked Susan.

"What do you children think?" asked Ulysses. "Is there such a thing as magic—I don't mean stage magic, but the real thing?"

Harold shrugged and looked uncertainly at Susan. "I guess not," she said slowly. "We had a talk about that in Sunday School because someone brought in a Ouija Board his aunt got him for his birthday. The teacher showed us a bunch of verses that said witchcraft was wrong. I don't know what's so bad about it, though."

"Well, just think about it. A magician is trying to control some power beyond himself—either demons, angels, or an impersonal power like the Force in *Star Wars*. Would God let you make one of His angels to obey you?"

"No," said the children together.

"Are you stronger than the devil?" The children shook their heads.

"The devil sometimes lets people think they can command his demons, but it's all a trick to lure them into his power. That leaves the Force. Is there a power in the universe that God doesn't control?"

Again the children shook their heads.

"Then how did we open the door into Earth-Two? If our words weren't magical, why did they cause the vortex to spin?" Harold frowned as he tried to think through the problem.

Ulysses paused. "Think of it this way. The door between our worlds is very heavy. It takes a great deal of energy to make it turn, but it is not a physical door; you can't push it with your hands. You have to push it with your minds. In my language, there is one word that enables me to focus the energy of my mind on going through the door. You did not know that word, but you used words from many languages to express your desire to enter through the door. Those words triggered something deep in your minds, and the energy came rushing out of you to push the door. That is the reason you were so tired and hungry. Your words did not compel some other power to obey you. Your words simply enabled you to use your own strength in a different way."

Pieces clicked together in Harold's head. "I think I understand," he said. Susan nodded her head in agreement. William said nothing, but he still looked puzzled.

By this time, the little group of tired explorers had come about two-thirds of the way down the canyon. Ulysses turned to the right and took them up over the ridge and down into the valley on the other side. It contained a small stream much like the one that ran beside their house. Ulysses led them up the stream into the deepening canyon. As the canyon began to narrow, the brush became thicker, and progress was slow. Ulysses, however, seemed to know every square inch of the way, and he expertly guided them along faint animal trails. When at last they reached the head of the canyon, their faces and hands were scratched, their clothes had a few tears, and their faces were etched with exhaustion.

The door, when they found it, was almost identical to their own familiar vortex. The only major difference, as William noted, was that the south end of his compass, rather than the north end, was drawn toward the hill.

Ulysses warned them again about the danger of coming back into Earth-Two. Then the four of them stood and held hands atop the mound. Ulysses spoke a single word, the hill began to spin, and the dense underbrush of Earth-Two was replaced by a dry, rocky gully in the children's own world. Ulysses took them to the bottom of the gully and said, "The road to your houses is straight ahead, about a hundred feet, I think. When you reach it, turn left. You should be home in an hour or so. Goodbye now, and remember what I told you."

Just before the children reached the road, they turned and looked for Ulysses. He was gone. As they trudged toward a belated dinner and a sure scolding, William voiced the questions that had occurred to all of them. "Do you guys want to go back to Earth-Two? And what are we going to tell our parents?"

CHAPTER 4—THE DISAPPEARANCE

Ｈow could you even think about going back?" demanded Susan. "Do you want to be trapped in Earth-Two?"

"No, of course not," replied William. "But I don't believe we would be trapped. Just stand still for a moment and think. Can you remember the word Ulysses used when he brought us through the door? Don't say it; just get it in mind. Susan, do you still have your notebook? Let's each write down what we remember and see if it is the same."

Susan produced the notebook and a pencil. They wrote by turns in silence, and then compared their answers. All three had written buhee. "I wonder what it means," said Harold.

"It doesn't matter what means! We are not going back!" insisted Susan. "And William, how could you even ask what we're going to tell our parents? We have to tell them everything."

The children argued all the way home. Harold and William called Susan a sissy and a chicken, which only made her even more determined to tell all. She stomped ahead of the boys, who looked at each other in dismay. Just before they reached home, Harold saw the wisdom of apologizing. "Susan! Susan! Wait up; I'm sorry. I shouldn't have called you names. You're my best friend. I don't want you to be angry at me."

"I'm sorry, too," said William, but his apology didn't sound quite as sincere as Harold's.

"Listen, Susan," said Harold. "Why don't we just postpone telling our parents for a day or two so that we can think things through? It won't hurt to wait a little bit, will it? William and I won't do anything without you; I promise. You promise, too, William." William promised, though a bit reluctantly, and

Susan agreed to wait at least until the next day.

That night, the Struthers children had cold spaghetti for supper. Their parents had already eaten, and Mrs. Struthers refused to reheat their food. It was a reminder, she said, for them to come home on time.

"What kept you?" she asked. "You look as though you have been playing in a briar patch. And why are you so glum? You haven't said more than two words to each other since you came home."

Susan looked down at her plate, so William spoke up quickly. "We came back a different way and, yes, there were some bushes with thorns and stickers on them. Then on the way home, we got into an argument, maybe because we were tired and hungry. But we made up, didn't we Susan?" Susan nodded her head and continued eating without looking up.

The next day, the members of the Ends of the Earth Explorers Club held an official meeting in their tree house. "Look at it this way," argued Harold. "As long as we are just gathering information, we aren't doing anything wrong. So let's see if we can find out what buhee means and what language it is. Then maybe we can convince our parents to let us go back."

"You know good and well that they will never say yes," countered Susan. "But I suppose it won't hurt for us to do some investigating. We can use the computer at the library to search the Internet. I wish we had a fast connection at home, but we're still stuck with dial-up."

And so they did, but none of the search engines gave any listing for buhee. Then they tried looking up buhee in all the foreign language dictionaries they could find—still nothing. They asked everyone they knew what the word might mean, but with no success.

When Mrs. Struthers wondered why they were interested in such an unusual word, Susan replied, "It's a club secret, Mom.

Is that okay?"

"Sure, honey," she replied, "I'm glad you and the boys are having so much fun together this summer."

Finally, a week after their discovery of Earth-Two, the boys refused to continue the search for buhee. The day was clear and warm, the perfect kind of day for playing outside. Harold and William were disgusted with their lack of success, so they decided to stay home and look for crawdads in the creek.

"Keep your finger out of their pincers this time, William," said Susan.

"I will," he replied. "I'm going put the net from our fish tank underneath them after I pull them up on the string."

Susan rode into town with her father when he went to work, and he picked her up at the library on his way home. As she passed William on her way into the house, she discreetly crossed the first fingers of her right and left hands to form an X—the secret sign to call for a meeting of the club. She smiled smugly at her brother, and when he raised his eyebrows in a question, she nodded her head. William ran off to catch Harold before he went in for supper.

After supper, the boys met in the tree house and waited in breathless excitement for Susan. It was her turn to wash dishes, and it seemed to be taking her forever.

"What's taking her so long?" asked Harold.

"Maybe Mom is making her do the cooking pots," answered William. "If the food is really stuck to the bottom of the pots, she sometimes lets us put them in the sink to soak until the food loosens up, but lots of times we have to scrub them anyway." He paused for a few seconds, and then added, "I think she is being slow on purpose. She does that sometimes when I'm in a hurry. She knows it makes me mad."

When Susan finally emerged from the kitchen, she strolled slowly toward the tree house. First, she stooped to pick a white-headed dandelion and scatter its seeds in the wind. Then, she peered down the old well at her reflection in the water.

"Susan! Hurry up!" shouted William.

Susan refused to hurry. She climbed slowly up the ladder to the platform in the branches and carefully settled down with her back against the trunk of the tree.

"What did you find out?" asked Harold. "You did call for a meeting didn't you?"

"Oh, I just thought you might wish that you had come into town with me. Then you could have been there when I made my great discovery. But perhaps you aren't interested. Would you like to tell me about the crawdads in the creek instead?"

"Stop it, Susan. Just tell us what you found!" demanded William.

"Well, it occurred to me that maybe we were not spelling buhee correctly. So I decided to try something different. When we entered Earth-Two, we strung together a bunch of words that meant 'in' or 'into.' So I guessed that Ulysses was saying something that meant 'out' in his language."

"That makes sense," said Harold.

William nodded as Susan continued, "I used the Internet to look for the word 'out' in all of the languages I could think of. Then I looked in the encyclopedia to find a list of more languages. The word we were spelling buhee is a Sanskrit word that means 'outside.' It is actually spelled bahiH. I found out that in some languages, such as Sanskrit, i sounds like our long e. The capital H tells us to breathe out heavily at the end of the word."

"What is Sanskrit? Where is it spoken?" asked Harold.

"Sanskrit is an ancient language of India. It is related to most of the modern European languages—English, French, German, Russian, Greek, and a whole lot more. But wait; it gets better. I also looked up the Sanskrit word for 'inside.' It is antaH, which is pronounced untuh. I think we might be able to get into Earth-Two with that one word. If we can, then we should be able to get out with bahiH. I say it's time to tell our parents everything. Maybe all seven of us can go together."

Harold looked at William. William looked at Harold. Then both of them looked at Susan, and together they cried, "No!"

"Listen, Susan," said Harold. "If we tell our parents, either they will think we're telling lies, or they will simply forbid us to try it. My mom is super cautious. She gets all bent out of shape when she thinks her baby is in danger. If we say anything to our parents, that will be the absolute end of our exploring."

The debate went on until bedtime and continued throughout the next two days. Then it was Sunday. The lesson in Sunday school was built around Ephesians 6:1–3, "Children, obey your parents in the Lord, for this is right. Honor your father and mother (which is the first commandment with a promise), so that it may be well with you, and that you may live long on the earth."

As the teacher was introducing the verse and the theme of the lesson, Susan gave Harold's foot a little kick. He turned, and she whispered, "You and William had better listen hard this morning."

That afternoon the children went out to sit by the stream and talk. William spoke up first. "Look at it this way. If we tell our parents about Earth-Two, and they say we can't go, then it would be wrong to sneak off anyway. But if we don't ask, then we won't be disobeying them. So I say we should just do it and not say anything."

"No," said Susan. "That's not right. If you know what Dad and Mom would tell you to do, and you do the opposite, then it's just the same as if you disobeyed a direct order."

"Let's put it to a vote of the club members," said William. "This is a democracy, and the majority rules. I vote that we go.

How about you, Harold?"

Harold looked troubled. He didn't like going against Susan, and deep down he knew that she was right, but finally he answered, "I vote we go."

"There," said William, "are you a member of this club or not? Are you going to rat on us, or will you go with us?"

Susan hung her head. When she looked up again, there were tears in her eyes, but she said quietly, "I'll go. But if we can't get in by saying antaH, we have to tell our parents. Okay?"

Monday was cold and rainy, but by Tuesday morning the sky had cleared, and the expedition set out for the vortex. Susan walked last in line with her head bowed and the words of Ephesians 6 echoing in her head, "Children obey your parents. Honor your father and mother." Most of the time she was crying softly.

By ten o'clock the children were standing at the top of the vortex hill, and by one minute after ten they had vanished.

That evening, they did not come home for supper. At eight o'clock, their fathers took flashlights and went out searching for them while Mrs. Struthers dialed 9–1–1. By six the next morning, teams of men with dogs had searched all of the nearby hills and valleys and found nothing.

CHAPTER 5—PIONEERS

Mrs. Wilson and Mrs. Struthers had spent the night in the kitchen. From time to time, two or three searchers would drop in for a cup of hot coffee and to report on their progress, but for the most part they were alone.

After one group of searchers had come and gone, Mrs. Wilson asked, "Is God listening to us? Will he bring my baby back? I have been pouring my heart out to Him, but I don't have any assurance that everything will be okay. What if they are already dead? Our prayers wouldn't do any good then." She put her face into her hands and began to cry.

Mrs. Struthers slid her chair around to the other side of the kitchen table so that she could put her arm around her friend's shoulders. For a long time, even after the tears ceased flowing down Mrs. Wilson's cheeks, her whole body continued to shake with dry, heaving sobs. When even those had stopped, Mrs. Struthers spoke. Her eyes were red from crying, but her voice was steady. "I don't know whether we will ever see our children in this life or not, but God wants us to trust in Him when we are afraid. All three of our children know Jesus Christ as their Savior. If something terrible has happened to them, they are not lost to us forever. They are safe in the arms of Jesus."

"I know," sniffed Mrs. Wilson, "I suppose we should tell our Father that we do trust Him."

And so the two mothers held hands and prayed, and then they dozed with their heads leaning on the kitchen table. They were awakened just as the sky was becoming gray instead of black. Their husbands and several other men were coming in for something to eat. The women fixed a hearty breakfast of eggs, pancakes and sausage, and then packed lunches for those who were going back to the search.

Two other crews came in later. Some of the ladies from their church also dropped by with more food. At ten o'clock that morning there was a lull in the activity, and Mrs. Wilson went out to get the mail from their two roadside boxes. When she returned, her face was pale, and her shaking hand was clutching a letter. "Here. This was in your box. It's from Susan. It has yesterday's post mark, so she must have put it in my box yesterday morning to be picked up and delivered to your box today."

Mrs. Struthers tore open the envelope and began to read, "Dear Mom and Dad, if we did not come home last night, I want you to know what has happened to us." The letter was five pages long. It gave a detailed account of the children's adventures and how they were planning to use the Sanskrit word antaH to open the door to Earth-Two. Susan even explained the proper pronunciation of antaH and their anticipated exit word, bahiH.

The two women looked at each other in silence for a full minute before Mrs. Wilson spoke. "Are you thinking what I'm thinking? We have to go after them."

"Yes," said her friend. "I don't think we should tell anybody but our husbands. People will think we're crazy or that our kids have cooked up a big practical joke and that they're hiding out in the woods someplace. William might do that, but not Susan."

"I agree Wendy, but what if we can't get back?" asked Mrs. Struthers. "How will we live? What will we eat? Are there any Earth-Two villages that would take us in? We could be stuck in the wilderness all by ourselves for a long time. I think we should try to take everything we'll need to be pioneers or settlers in a new land. Are you ready for that?"

Wendy Wilson sighed. "Yes, Sharon, but I don't even know where to begin. We'll need so much stuff, and how are we going to carry it all?"

"I have an idea," said her friend. She pulled out her cell phone and punched in a number. "Hello, Mr. Larson. This is Sharon Struthers. We live down at the old Rogers's place. Yes, that's right. We are the family whose children have disappeared. No, I didn't see it on the morning news. We didn't even think of turning on the television. I'm calling because I understand you have a donkey for sale. We are afraid the children have gone much farther than the rescuers think. We have an idea of where they might be, and we thought the donkey could carry our supplies while we looked. Yes, I know that the forest behind our house extends for hundreds of square miles. Yes, I know it might be like hunting for a needle in a haystack. No, I don't want to borrow the donkey. I want to buy it. Do you happen to have a packsaddle with pouches for carrying baggage? Good, I'd like to buy that as well. Can we get the donkey today? Do you have a trailer? Good. That's great! I'll be down to help you load him in about twenty minutes."

Mrs. Struthers clicked the phone off and then on again. This time she called Myrtle, a friend from church, and arranged for her daughter to stay in the house. The girl was home from college and had not been able to find a summer job. She was glad to be paid to watch over both houses, keep the grass mown, and be present in case the children should wander back home.

By nightfall, the two women had purchased four sleeping bags, four backpacks, two tents, freeze-dried food, garden seeds, a two-man saw for felling trees, a first-aid kit, and everything else they thought might be helpful. They used the donkey to carry the first load of tools and supplies to the vortex. They planned to leave most of the heavier items on the other side of the vortex in Earth-Two until after they found the children. If they could not return to Earth, they would use these things to build a new home and feed themselves through the first winter.

Late that evening when their exhausted husbands finally came home for supper, the two women explained their plans.

"Wendy, that is just crazy," said her husband. "Sam and I will go after the kids by ourselves. If we don't come back in a day or so, you can come in after us."

"And how are we supposed to find you once we get there?" she replied. "If Earth-Two has lots of dangerous animals, how do you expect us to defend ourselves while we're wandering around looking for you? No! If you're going, I'm going, too."

The two couples argued for over an hour, but finally the men gave in to their wives. The next morning, the men made one last trip to the hardware store while the women packed, so it was nearly noon by the time the four of them headed up the canyon to the vortex. Each of them carried personal items and clothing in a backpack. The donkey was loaded with as much camping equipment and food as it could carry.

When they arrived, they gathered in a circle around the donkey and the first load of supplies that the women had left there the day before. It was quite a stretch, but they managed to hold hands as together they repeated the Sanskrit word for inside—antaH. The ground trembled and began to spin. When they opened their eyes a few moments later, the smaller trees of Earth-One had been replaced by the forest giants of Earth-Two.

"Wow! It really happened. We're here," said Mr. Struthers. "I kept hoping that the letter was a practical joke, even though I was sure Susan would never agree to such a trick. I'm starved, just like Susan said they were when they pushed through the vortex door. I guess we can eat granola bars while we walk."

The little party headed down the canyon. After thirty minutes of somber silence, Mr. Struthers, who was leading the way, stopped and pointed at the ground to his right. "That looks like a tennis shoe track, Susan's I think. This must be where they turned to go up over the hill."

The parents turned to follow a winding animal trail up over the hill that separated them from the next valley. As they neared the ridge of the hill, Mrs. Struthers cried out, "Oh, no! Look!" A bright splotch of pink and purple was visible among the thorny branches of a wild rose bush. "That's Susan's school backpack!"

And indeed it was. The strong nylon fabric was all shredded as if it had been raked by giant claws. Susan's mother pulled the pack out of the bush, clutched it to her chest and began to cry. In her mind's eye a giant cat-like creature was tearing her daughter to shreds. What she would have seen two days earlier was much different.

* * * *

Susan was last in line as Harold led the adventurers up that same path. Without warning, rough hands reached out from behind a bush she had just passed and seized her left arm. With a shriek, she twisted away, but as she turned to flee, the hands grabbed her backpack. Susan slipped her arms through the straps and ran. She tore through the brush on the right side of the trail, jumped over a log and was off like a deer, but even a deer can sometimes be run down by a wolf. A hundred yards into the forest, the rough hands grabbed her again. Her captor swung her around, hoisted her in the air and slung her over his shoulder as easily as if she had been a large, stuffed doll. He growled something in a language Susan did not understand, but she was too out of breath and too terrified to answer.

By the time they reached the trail again, the two boys were both tied by their wrists, with a choking leash around their necks. Harold was bleeding from a large cut in his lower lip, and a nasty bump was beginning to grow on William's forehead. Soon Susan was bound in the same fashion, and their captors began leading them toward the top of the ridge.

The group that held them prisoner consisted of four men and four women. They were all fair-skinned (though tanned), with blue eyes and light brown to golden hair. Three of the men held the children's leashes while the fourth seemed to be barking orders.

"You OK, Susan," asked Harold?

She nodded. "You and William don't look too good."

The leader of band turned, glared at the children and said something harsh. A golden-haired woman, who had been walking beside them, put one finger to her lips and shook her head, so after that they walked in silence.

As they descended into the valley on the other side of the ridge, Susan noticed that the leader was looking carefully at the ground and at the bushes on either side of the game trail. When they turned toward the head of the canyon, his investigation became more intense, and their progress became slower. After a few minutes, he stopped and pointed at some broken twigs and a bit of cloth that had torn from William's shirt on their first visit. He whispered a quiet order and the whole group stopped, except for one of the women who crouched down and began sneaking through the underbrush toward the exit vortex.

When she returned a few minutes later, she whispered one word, "Odysseus."

Susan's heart skipped a beat: *Odysseus...Ulysses...might he have two names? Who else would be here besides him?* Susan mouthed, "Ulysses" to Harold and then raised her eyebrows in a silent question. Harold shrugged. Then he pursed his lips in a silent, "Shh." A few seconds later that warning became entirely unnecessary when a ball of cloth was stuffed into their mouths and held in place by a strip of leather tied at the back of their necks. The small band moved forward again, even more slowly than before, but this time the woman with hair of yellow gold held all their leashes and kept them a few yards behind the rest of the group.

Just before they reached the clearing at the head of the canyon, the leader motioned for the woman to bring the children up beside him. The remaining men and women spread out into the forest on either side of the trail. Soon they were hidden by the trees, but when they reached the clearing they all stepped into the open together, forming a semi-circle around the vortex mound. On top of the mound was Ulysses.

He stood tall and straight with his color-shifting cloak stirring in the breeze. He seemed perfectly relaxed and apparently unconcerned about the fact that he was vastly outnumbered. To Susan's surprise, he gave no hint that he recognized the children. Harsh words were spoken by the leader of the children's captors. Stern, calm words, potent with authority, came from the lips of Ulysses.

As if by a pre-arranged signal, the men and women, who had captured the children, raised their arms toward Ulysses and shouted. Instantly large stones and clods of earth erupted from the ground and flew toward him. Instinctively, Susan staggered backward until the leash around her neck tightened cutting off her air. She panicked and struggled briefly against the noose, but that only made it worse.

By the time she recovered and looked back at the vortex, calm had settled. Ulysses was standing relaxed on top of the mound with piles of rubble around the base. A slight smile was on his lips. With open palms extended as a gesture of peace, he spoke a few quiet words.

The leader of his opponents shouted something in return and the battle resumed. For the next few minutes shouts and wild gestures from the enemies of Ulysses sent stones, lightning bolts, and waves of flame against him. Nothing touched him. It seemed as if he was surrounded by an invisible wall. Although he was no longer smiling, he remained unmoved. He did not speak or wave his arms. A simple glance at one of his enemies was enough to send a skull-crushing boulder back at the assailant who had sent it. Unlike Ulysses, his opponents were scrambling as they dodged or deflected his attacks.

Finally, Ulysses raised his right arm, and with a broad sweeping motion spoke a forest fire into existence half a mile below them. Flames filled the valley from ridge to ridge and a gentle breeze began to funnel the blaze up toward the end of the box canyon where they all stood.

The leader of their captors looked grim. He spoke a few quiet words to the woman who held their leashes. She nodded, passed the leashes to him, and ran first left and then right to whisper a message into the ears of her comrades. When she returned, the whole group raised their arms to the canyon walls and shouted with one voice. Then they turned and fled toward the flames dragging the children behind them. A mighty rumble like the sound of a hundred freight trains filled the air. The ground shook under their feet, and Susan looked back to see the walls of the canyon collapsing down on the lone figure of Ulysses.

Susan ran until she thought her lungs would burst. How, she wondered, would they ever pass through the wall of fire ahead? The answer came when they were less than a hundred yards from the flames. At that point, the stream they were following flowed into a broad, deep pool. The golden-haired woman removed their gags and leashes and shoved them into the water. Floating or standing with just their noses above the water, they waited until the fire swept past them.

When they emerged from the water, the woman tied ropes around their waists instead of their necks. "That's some improvement," said Harold. William nodded glumly.

"Do you think he's dead," asked Susan? She didn't want to

use Ulysses' name for fear that their captors might realize they knew him.

"Dunno," said Harold.

And then they were off, down through the charred ruins of the valley, and then climbing the steep ridge to their right, farther and farther from home. When they reached the top, all breathless and sweating, the whole party looked back. The fire had mostly burned itself out for lack of fuel at the head of the canyon. Nothing moved in the pile of rubble where Ulysses had stood.

With anguish in her heart and fury in her voice, Susan screamed at the leader of their captors, "Our parents are coming. They are coming! And they will find us!"

With a slap, he knocked her to the ground.

CHAPTER 6—THE PURSUIT

Mr. Struthers put his arms around his wife and held her close. He did not cry, but his face was very grim. Finally, he said. "Come on, Sharon. There's no real evidence that Susan was hurt. Maybe she dropped her pack and it was found later by some wild beast. At any rate, we can't stay here. We must go on. Just keep remembering what God's Word says, 'When I am afraid, I will put my trust in You.'"

Mrs. Struthers nodded, blew her nose on a tissue and said, "I'm ready now."

A few minutes later they were standing at the top of the ridge, looking down. What they saw was not a valley full of dense brush, as Susan's letter had described it, but a scene of terrifying devastation. Most of the bushes had been burned; some were still smoldering, and the stream flowing through the valley ran black with ash. A few large trees had been uprooted, and farther up at the head of the canyon, a giant rockslide covered the area where the exit vortex should have been. With a growing tightness in their throats, four anxious parents descended into the valley and began to pick their way through the charred wasteland toward the rockslide.

As they neared the head of the canyon, a tall figure rose up out of the rubble and stood to wait for them. His shirt and pants were forest green, but his color-shifting cape seemed to blend in with his surroundings. Mrs. Wilson rushed forward and stood trembling before him. "Are you Ulysses? Have you seen my baby, my Harold? Where are the children? Are they buried beneath those rocks? Are they dead?"

"Yes, I am Ulysses. No, the children are not dead. They have been captured and taken as hostages."

"Hostages? What do you mean? Is someone demanding a ransom for them? Are their lives in danger?"

"Slow down, Mrs. Wilson. You are Mrs. Wilson, are you not?" replied Ulysses. "I will do the best I can to answer your questions, but let's get moving. They have two days head start on us. We can talk as we walk. By the way, do you have anything I can eat? I haven't had much since the battle that spoiled this beautiful valley."

Ulysses ate two large ham sandwiches, an apple, and a Mars Bar as he listened to their story and read Susan's letter. Then he reported what had happened when the children reached the valley as prisoners. "I was expecting that band of rebels," he continued, "but I had no way to anticipate that your children would stumble into their path. Those men and women were attempting to escape from our world into yours. The words that open the doors between the worlds are quite simple, but they have been kept secret by our ruling council. The rebels hoped to camp by this isolated vortex, trying everything they could think of until they succeeded. I was sent to stop them."

"Then why didn't you go after them," asked Sharon Struthers, "and why didn't you try to rescue our children?"

"Because I was waiting for you. As I lay under the pile of rocks in a protective bubble, I extended a listening tube through the rubble. If I had heard the rebels return, I would have been prepared to surprise them. What I heard instead was a distant wail from Susan, 'Our parents are coming! They will rescue us."

"Well, we have come," said Mr. Wilson, "but I don't suppose we will be of much use against the kind of power that ruined the vortex valley."

"Maybe not, Fred, but I will teach you as much as I can while we travel. Perhaps you will be of some use. At any rate you need to learn how to protect yourselves from the saber-toothed cats."

When Ulysses mentioned saber-toothed cats, Mrs. Wilson

shrieked and began to collapse. She would have fallen to the ground if her husband had not caught her.

"Thank you for being willing to teach us," said Mr. Struthers. "By the way, where are we going?"

"To the next-nearest exit vortex. I followed them far enough to be sure of that. It will take them a couple of weeks to reach the general vicinity, but I don't think they know exactly where it is. I will take you by a shorter way. The rebels know that your children are not from our world, so they must assume that they know the passwords between the worlds. I believe they hope to extract that information from the children when they reach their destination."

"Susan's letter said that the passwords were in Sanskrit. Is that the language you speak here?" asked Mrs. Struthers.

"No, Sharon. Sanskrit is an ancient language from your perspective, but the language we speak is far older. It is the mother of all languages. Sanskrit contains some words from the Mother Tongue. *BahiH* and *antaH* are among them.

"The mother of all languages—was that the language of Adam and Eve? How can you still speak it? I thought that language was lost when God scattered the nations after the tower of Babel."

"It was lost from your Earth, Sharon, but God had already created our world, Earth-Two, as a place to preserve it. The Mother Tongue is a marvelously rich and complex language. When God confused the tongues of the rebels, he did not create a different language for each group. Instead He gave each group a piece of the Mother Tongue and made them forget the rest."

"I took Spanish in high school," muttered Mr. Wilson, "but it didn't take any special act of God to make me forget it. I did that all on my own." The other parents and Ulysses chuckled.

"The mother of all languages was like a great tree with many branches," continued Ulysses. "God broke branches from that great language tree, and gave a branch to every tribe. Naturally, those branches have continued to grow and develop, but every modern language still retains part of the Mother Tongue. Some of the words and the basic grammar of every tongue are related to the mother."

"So God created this earth as a place to preserve the Mother Tongue?" asked Mrs. Wilson. "Wow! How cool is that?"

"Yes, and He created doors between the worlds because He didn't want us to lose contact with the rest of the human race. I think He especially wanted us to know about the death and resurrection of Christ so that we could believe and be saved."

"Is the Mother Tongue what enabled you to hurl rocks and start fires without touching anything?" asked Mr. Struthers. "And is that what you are going to teach us?"

"Yes to both questions, Sam, but you won't learn very much in the time we have. Only a very few of our people have mastered our language as thoroughly as I have. If your children had not been captured by the rebels, I would have had no difficulty dealing with them. The oldest of them can't be more than sixty years old—hardly long enough to learn very much apart from the intensive training that rangers receive."

"If sixty is young, does that mean you're old?" asked Mrs. Struthers. "Somehow you look both young and old at the same time."

"Yes, Sharon, I am what you would call old. I have seen four hundred and seventy-three summers. As I said, the mother of all languages is very complex. God gave the whole language to Adam when he created him, but we must learn it over time. We teach the basics to all of our children, but mastering the language requires specialized teaching techniques and many years of intensive study. I am a ranger, trained and authorized by the ruling council of my world to defend the weak and maintain justice in the territory assigned to me. In addition, my body has become hard and strong through my many years of wandering. I have reserves of strength and energy that are uncommon even among my people—and we have no couch potatoes here. "

Mr. Wilson looked down at his overly large waist and sighed. "If we have several days of hiking ahead of us, maybe I won't be a couch potato by the time we get back."

As they talked, the searchers had been following the course of the stream down the valley. Ulysses led them across it at a shallow place where large rocks served as stepping-stones. Mr. Wilson, who had been leading the donkey, was on the next-to the last rock when the animal decided he needed a drink. The donkey pulled at the halter-rope, and down went Mr. Wilson. When he climbed out, he was wet to his waist. Ashes and silt from the battle upstream clung to his jeans. Mrs. Wilson bit her lower lip trying to stifle a laugh.

"I sure wouldn't want to drink that stuff," he said as he hauled the donkey away from the water. "That critter must not have any taste buds. If he doesn't become more cooperative, we will never catch up to our kids."

* * * *

As their parents were walking and talking with Ulysses, Harold, Susan, and William were being dragged farther and farther from home. Their feet were sore and swollen, their throats were parched from thirst, and they were very hungry.

Shortly after noon, they stopped briefly beside a small stream. The woman with the golden hair motioned for them to drink. The water was so cold it made their teeth hurt. Harold stuck his whole face into the quiet pool and splashed water over his hair. "That feels better," he said. "I thought I was going to die from the heat!"

After Susan and William had followed Harold's example, the young woman motioned for them to get up. William refused, and the man who was in charge shouted at him and gave him a sharp kick in the side.

"William!" screamed Susan. The young woman grabbed her arm, but Susan jerked away and knelt beside her brother. Tears pooled in his eyes, and his breath came in short painful gasps, but he didn't cry. Susan and Harold helped him to his feet but he was in so much pain that he could hardly stand.

The young woman untied the rope from William's waist. Then she placed both hands on his side and said a few quiet words that he didn't understand. When she motioned for him to follow her, he found he was able to walk . A few minutes later, he moved up between Harold and Susan, and said, "I don't know what she did, but it helped. I still hurt some, but it's not as bad. Anyway, I think I can keep up. Why didn't she tie me up again?"

"What would you do if you managed to escape by yourself?" asked Harold. "None of us knows where we are or how to get home. Besides, do really you think you could outrun these people?"

"No, I suppose not. I think maybe she likes me. Anyway, she's not as mean as that other guy."

Supper that night was a small bowl of soup and a dry biscuit. The children ate greedily, even though it didn't taste very good. Then, bound hand and foot, they huddled together under a large tree.

"What should we do? I don't think I can stand another day like the last two," said William. He began to cry. Susan did the best she could to draw her little brother close to her. She held him so that his head rested on her chest until he became calmer.

"I suppose we could pray," said Harold, "but I think God must be pretty mad at us for not honoring our parents and for sneaking through the vortex door without their permission. He probably won't listen to us."

"Yes He will," replied Susan. "All three of us are God's children. He wants us to come to Him, even when we've been bad. Our parents taught us a neat verse, 1 John 1:9. 'If we confess our sins, He is faithful and righteous to forgive us our sins and to cleanse us from all unrighteousness.' Harold, if we confess our sins to God right now, then we can pray and ask Him to help us."

And that is what they did.

CHAPTER 7—TRUST

Ulysses was laughing. He laughed so hard he had to sit down on a log to recover his breath. When he could speak again, he said, "You should see yourselves! You are very funny! Have you ever put up a tent before? Have you ever even slept outside in your own backyard?" The Wilsons and the Strutherses shook their heads. "Here, let me help you. I don't use a tent, but I have seen them in your world, and this kind is really quite simple."

By the time they had finished setting up camp, it was nearly dark. Ulysses called them over to a fire ring made of rocks. In the center of the ring, he had carefully placed a small pile of twigs. He pointed to the twigs with his first finger and spoke two words. Immediately, the little pile began to burn.

"Wow!" exclaimed Mr. Wilson.

"Do you want to try it?" asked Ulysses as he scattered the fire with a stick.

"You bet," he answered, but on his first three tries, nothing happened. The fourth time, he managed to set his shoelaces on fire, and the other parents laughed. His fifth and sixth attempts were both successful, but by then Mr. Wilson was so tired that he couldn't even stand up.

"Now it's your turn, Sam," said Ulysses.

It took him five tries before he got a little smoke from his pile of dried leaves and twigs. "I guess I shouldn't have been so quick to laugh at you, Fred," he said.

Both mothers started their small fires in only three tries. Mr. Struthers looked a little put out until his wife said, "Don't fret, Sam. Wendy and I got to watch you and Fred before we tried it. I'm sure that helped us learn that trick a little faster."

With their lesson for the evening over, Ulysses allowed the parents to eat supper and tumble into bed. As Mr. Struthers drifted off to sleep, he thought he could hear Ulysses out in the woods speaking in a strange language, and then he dreamed that Ulysses was answered by something that sounded like a cross between a growl and a purr. He asked the other parents about it in the morning, but none of them had heard anything.

* * * *

Early the next morning and several miles away, Harold, Susan, and William were awakened by a quiet voice and a gentle shake. The same young woman who had eased William's pain was bending over them. She untied their ropes and took them down to a nearby stream to wash. When they returned to camp, Harold pointed at their bonds, rubbed his sore, chaffed wrists and shook his head. The young woman smiled, put the ropes into her own pack, and gave them each a hard biscuit for breakfast.

She walked beside them all that day. Her name, they learned, was Frigga. She had bright blue eyes, hair the color of yellow gold and a quick, contagious smile. When she laughed, her voice sounded like the gentle bubbling of a clear mountain stream. Harold and William liked her immediately. Susan was suspicious.

Frigga worked hard at learning English. She was very quick, and by the end of the day she could string together the words she had learned into simple sentences.

After supper, the man who had kicked William roughly bound their hands and feet together and secured them to the base of a large tree. Frigga came over after he had finished. She pointed at the ropes and said, "I sorry." Tossing her head in the direction of the man who had tied them up, she said, "Hagen think you run away." Then she laid a blanket over them, touched their cheeks gently and left.

That night, Harold dreamed about Frigga. He saw himself and Frigga walking hand in hand through a quiet mountain meadow. The next morning as they were chewing a chunk of stale bread for breakfast, Harold shared his dream with William.

Susan, who was sitting a few feet away grunted, "Humph! I dreamed about Frigga too, but in my dream she turned into a snarling wolf with long, sharp teeth."

* * *

"At least a hare's teeth aren't as sharp as the teeth of the wolf we heard last night," said Mr. Wilson as he inched slowly toward the rabbit-like creature.

"Just because he nipped Sam doesn't mean you have to be afraid of him, Fred," said his wife. "Go ahead. Stretch out your hand and say his name, *arnebeth*."

"*Arnebeth, arnebeth,* nice little *arnebeth*" said Fred. "OUCH! He bit me, too. I thought saying its name in the Mother Tongue was supposed to keep it from attacking me."

"He didn't attack you, honey. You went toward him, but I think he sensed that you were nervous, and he didn't trust you. Is that right, Ulysses?"

"Yes," said Ulysses. "You and Sharon seem to have a knack for putting animals at ease. Why don't you play with the hare while I bring in something a little bigger."

Sharon knelt down, stretched out both hands toward the hare and spoke as gently as if she had been talking to a child, "*Arnebeth, arnebeth,* come to me." When the furry little creature hopped over, she picked it up and then sat down on a nearby log. "Come on Sam; come on Fred. You pet him while I talk to him."

Fifteen minutes later when Ulysses returned to the campsite, Fred was holding and petting the *arnebeth*.

"You'd better send the *arnebeth* away now. Even though he

isn't frightened of you any more, Fred, he would be terrified of our next guest.

Mrs. Wilson picked up the hare from her husband's arms, carried it to the opposite side of the clearing, and set it down. A little pat on its rear end sent it bouncing off into the brush.

When she turned around, Ulysses was leading into the clearing the largest cat-like creature she had ever seen. Its tawny head reached to his shoulder, and although it was a little shorter in length than the lions in the zoo and only had a short bobtail, it looked heavier, stronger, and fiercer. A long fang protruded down from each side of its mouth.

The two men quickly pushed their wives behind them and backed away from the beast.

"Don't worry," chuckled Ulysses. "I don't expect you to get close to one of these saber-toothed cats. "I just want you to be able to say its name correctly so that it won't attack you. In our ancient tongue it is *shachal. Shachal*—now you try it."

After all four parents practiced the word several times, Susan looked at Wendy with a bit of a grin and a shrug of her shoulders. Wendy smiled back and nodded. Then the two mothers began walking toward Ulysses and the great cat, speaking its name as they slowly approached. On their lips, *shachal* sounded like a gentle purr, as if a mother cat were soothing her kittens. The saber-tooth, which had been standing stiffly beside Ulysses, began to relax.

Ulysses kept his hand on the shoulders of the great beast until the two women reached him and began to pet it. Then he stepped aside. As Susan and Wendy continued petting and speaking quietly to the *shachal*, it sank slowly to the ground, rested its great head on Susan's left foot, and went to sleep.

Ulysses shook his head in amazement. "I've never seen such a thing. I've heard of it, but never witnessed it before."

Mr. Struthers looked at Mr. Wilson and said, "I guess our

wives get an A in the Mother-Tongue class, and we get a C."

"Or maybe a D," groaned Mr. Wilson. "I certainly feel like a Dunce."

"Don't be so hard on yourselves," said Ulysses. "I think you two will soon be moving earth and stone with the Mother Tongue better than your wives will ever be able to manage. The four of you are quite gifted. I would never have expected as much from people who did not grow up speaking our ancient language."

"I think it will be a long time before we can carry on a conversation in the Mother Tongue," said Mrs. Wilson. "Will these few words and tricks we have learned really help when we catch up to our children?"

"Only our God knows, Wendy" replied the ranger, "but my heart tells me that it may make the difference between life and death. We shall just have to wait and see."

* * * *

Day by day, the rebels led their captives farther from their home through the ancient forests of Earth-Two. Most of one day they followed a clear trail, but the rest of the time Hagen seemed to be choosing his path by looking at the shapes of the hills, the valleys, and the rivers. As the days passed, Frigga became more fluent in English, and the children were able to talk to her more easily.

In the beginning, her words were often in the wrong order: "Parents have you? School, there do you go? House big is it?" The children usually understood what she meant, and after a while she was doing better.

"What does your father do for a living, Harold?"

"Oh, he sells insurance."

"Insurance? That's a new word. What does it mean?"

"Well, if your house burns down, your insurance company pays to have people rebuild it for you."

"Why would they do that?" asked Frigga. "Wouldn't your neighbors all come together and help you put up a new one?"

"No," said Harold. "Wait, here's another example. If your car was in an accident—"

"What's a car?" interrupted Frigga.

Describing cars took the three children the better part of an hour.

"Oh, my brain is tired," said William. "Why don't you talk for a while? Tell us about your home and your family. Better yet, tell us where we're going and why."

Frigga pressed her pretty lips into a decidedly unpretty frown. Then she shook her head and strode ahead of the children.

That night, after they had been tied up as usual, Susan wiggled as close as she could to William and Harold. "Are you boys blind? Can't you see what she's doing?" she whispered. "She asks questions but never answers them. She wants to know all about us, but tells us nothing about herself. There's something she wants from us. I don't know what it is yet, but we have to be careful. Remember, God wants us to be as wise as serpents and as harmless as doves. So cooperate with her, but don't tell her anything important. She knows we came from Earth-One, but don't let on that this is our second time here, and don't tell her we know Ulysses. I think she already suspects that we do."

"You just don't like her because she's so pretty," said William. "I think she's really nice. If it weren't for that monster, Hagen, I bet she would make things a lot easier for us."

"Humph!" grunted Susan. "Anyway, don't tell her about Ulysses. Now goodnight." She wiggled around a bit to move her shoulder away from an uncomfortable root and closed her eyes, but she did not fall asleep right away. Something was very wrong, but she didn't know what it was.

The next morning as soon as they were on their way, Frigga said, "I am glad we were able to rescue you from Odysseus. If we had not been there, who knows what he might have done to you." As she spoke, Susan noticed that Frigga seemed to be watching them with special interest.

She's looking for something, thought Susan. I wonder what.

The children did not respond, so Frigga went on, "Odysseus is the man who was fighting us back in the valley where we found you. We have never met him before, but we have heard many stories about his evil deeds." Again, Frigga looked carefully at their faces.

"Frigga," began William, "I don't think—" At that point Susan stumbled and fell, crashing into both William and Harold. As the three children picked themselves up from the ground, Susan, with her back turned toward Frigga, scowled at William and mouthed the words, "Be wise."

"What don't you think?" asked Frigga after they had dusted themselves off.

"I, uh, I uh don't think we could have defended ourselves. I'm glad you protected us." William did not sound very convincing. Frigga looked hard at him, but said nothing.

"If we were being rescued," said Susan, "why did you tie us up? And why are we still tied up every night?"

"None of us knew English, so we could not explain the danger you were in. We were afraid for our lives, but we wanted to save you as well, so we had to bring you along by force. Hagen insists on tying you up at night because he doesn't want you to wander off and be eaten by some wild animal. I suppose you have heard them growling out there in the darkness."

The children nodded; they had been frightened several times by the night noises of the forest. "Hagen may seem to be very rough, but he has a kind heart. He is leading us to a place where you can get back into your own world."

The rest of the day, Harold and William talked excitedly about the prospect of going home. Susan was privately worried that their parents might have followed the instructions in her letter and were trapped in Earth-Two with no way out, but she didn't want to dampen the boys' hopes, so she didn't say anything. In any event, there was nothing they could do.

That evening after supper, as Hagen walked toward the children with a rope in his hand, Frigga stepped up and stood in front of him. She pointed toward the children and shook her head. Hagen shouted something at her and made as if to walk around her, but she moved to block his way again.

"What's going on?" whispered William,

"I think Frigga's trying to keep him from tying us up," said Susan.

Hagen snarled something that would sound like a curse in any language. He looked as if he might strike Frigga, but one of the other men grabbed his arm. Hagen glared at him for several seconds, and then he turned toward Frigga and spat in her face. After that he stomped off to the other side of the camp.

Frigga rubbed her sleeve across her face and then went to kneel beside William who was shaking uncontrollably. "It's okay, William. Hagen has a temper, to be sure, but he is not a bad man. Most of the time he is an inspiring leader. Now go to sleep, all of you. There really is no sense in tying you up at night. After all, where would you go?"

That night, the children lay down for the first time without being roped to a tree. When Susan was sure they were alone, she whispered, "William, you almost blew it. Frigga knew that you didn't finish what you meant to say. You were going to tell her his name wasn't Odysseus, and that he had been kind to us, weren't you?"

"Well so what if I was? I don't think that would hurt anything. Frigga is our friend. She'll take us home. Maybe

Ulysses would have killed us. He told us not to come back to Earth-Two. Maybe he is evil. Why did he lie to us about his name? Anyway, he must be dead, so what difference would it make?"

"He didn't lie to us about his name, William," said Harold. "Don't you remember? He told us, 'You may *call* me Ulysses, the wanderer.' He didn't *say* that was his real name. Maybe he has a reason for using different names. Maybe he has a secret identity, like Superman. I like Frigga as much as you do, but when she said that Ulysses is evil and that Hagen has a kind heart—well, that just didn't ring true. Hagen is mean. Have you forgotten how hard he kicked you? He didn't act the least bit sorry for that. Ulysses was a little stern, but he really did care what happened to us. I felt a deep-down goodness when we were with him. I don't feel that way about any of these people, even Frigga. Of course, if he is dead...."

William started to answer, but Susan cut him short. "Please," she said, "let's not fight. We have to stick together. Each of us has his own opinion, but none of us really knows what's going on.

"How are we ever going to figure out who's telling us the truth and whom we can trust?" asked Harold. "Maybe we'd better pray and ask God to guide us and to keep us from making any terrible mistakes."

And that is what they did.

CHAPTER 8—THROUGH THE WILDERNESS

I know," said Harold the next morning. "Let's ask Frigga whether she is a Christian or not. If she is, then I'll feel better about trusting her. I thought of something else, too. She's never met Ulysses, so maybe she believes he's evil because friends like Hagen over there have told her that he is."

"What if she lies and says yes?" asked Susan. "Still, I can't think of anything better. Maybe God has answered our prayer for wisdom by giving you that idea. I suppose we could give it a try. What do you think, William?" Susan asked.

"Okay and I think I should be the one to ask her. If you ask her, Susan, she may suspect a trap, but she knows I like her. Besides, I think she probably is a Christian already."

William's opportunity came later that afternoon. Frigga had been asking questions about their life on Earth-One. Harold was describing their school and their church, and Susan, who sensed that an opening might be coming, began to pray silently. At a pause in the conversation, William asked with sincere and cheerful confidence, "Are you a Christian, too, Frigga? What is your church like?"

Frigga's face clouded over, and it was several seconds before she replied. "No, I'm not a Christian. That belief is fine for children and old folks, like my parents, but it's no good for people like my friends and me. We don't need any religion, or want it."

"Frigga," said Susan gently, "that doesn't even make sense. If Christianity is true, then it is good for you as well as for kids and old people. If it's not true, then it can't be good for kids because it won't prepare them for life. And if it's not true, then it's not good for old people either. Why should they use the last years of their lives trying to please a God who doesn't exist?" Susan looked Frigga full in the face, not defiantly, but calmly, steadily, and with genuine concern. Finally, Frigga turned her face away and pushed on ahead of the children to walk by herself.

Susan looked over at William. Big tears were trickling slowly down his cheeks. Susan took his hand and walked quietly beside him for some time. After a while, Harold stepped around them and moved up to walk beside Frigga so he could talk to her. When they stopped briefly for lunch, Harold came back to his friends. "I was telling her what a big difference it made in our family when my dad became a Christian," he said. "At least she was willing to listen to me."

As often as possible over the next few days, the children returned to the topic of their faith in Christ. They also tried to ask Frigga about her family. On these occasions her naturally cheerful disposition retreated like the sun hiding behind a cloud. Normally, she tried to deflect the conversation to other subjects, but one time she exploded. "Of course I love my parents! They just didn't understand the important work that Hagen and the rest of us have to do. When Hagen came to our village recruiting support for his project, my parents said all kinds of bad things about him. Then, when I decided to follow him, they were furious. I left without saying goodbye."

"What is your project, Frigga?" asked Harold. But Frigga just pressed her lips together and would say no more on the subject.

"Frigga," asked Harold after a few minutes, "Are you really happy? I mean deep down in your heart? You seem to be carrying a heavy load. I learned a verse recently that might help you." With a glance toward Susan, he continued, "Jesus said, 'Come to Me, all who are weary and heavy-laden, and I will give you rest.' It's from Matthew chapter eleven. I think you're burdened and unhappy because of the way you left your parents. And maybe you're burdened because part of you still knows that Christ is God. Why don't you come to Him?"

"Thank you for your concern, Harold, but you just don't understand. I can't go back now, even if I wanted to." She paused and then added softly, "My parents taught me that verse when I was a child. It seems so long ago. Now go back and join your friends. I really don't want to talk anymore."

The next day, shortly before noon, they came to a deep gorge with a rushing river at the bottom. The whole group gathered at the edge looking for a place to cross. "That's a steep drop to the river," said Susan. "I hope Hagen doesn't make us climb down. I don't think I can make it, and I'm sure I can't swim through those rapids."

"It doesn't look any better up or down stream for as far as I can see," answered Harold. "We're standing at the narrowest part, and it must be sixty feet across."

"Sixty feet? How can you tell?" asked William.

"The apartment building where we used to live had six stories. My dad said each story was about ten feet high, so that made it sixty feet high. This gap looks about as wide as our apartment was tall."

As the children were talking, Hagen was eyeing a very tall, very straight pine tree that stood about ten feet from the gorge. He said something to Frigga, who called the children to join her some distance behind the tree. Then he and the other men stood shoulder to shoulder between the children and the tree. They raised their arms with their palms toward the tree and began to chant four words over and over.

"It looks as if they're pushing the tree, but they're not even touching it," said William.

"Shh," answered Frigga, with one finger to her lips.

At first, nothing happened, but gradually the tree began to tilt toward the gorge. Then, with the sound of a hundred bed sheets being torn apart at once, the roots of the giant tree were ripped from the ground. Before the tree could pick up speed, the men turned their hands around and began a different chant."

"Now it looks as if they are holding it back," said William.

"Shh," said Frigga.

With words of power, the four men gradually lowered the tree until its top came to rest well across the gorge.

"Wow!" exclaimed William. Frigga didn't say anything.

Next Hagen sent one of the women to clear a path across the big log. When she touched a branch and spoke to it, the branch simply detached itself from the trunk and fell into the water below. Within ten minutes, she had removed most of the branches on the upper side of the tree, leaving only those that would provide a good handhold.

Four men and three women crossed with apparent ease, leaving Frigga and the children. Harold went first, followed closely by Susan. They had only gone a little way when Harold heard Susan's quavering voice behind him. "I can't do this, Harold. It's so far down!"

"Well, don't look down."

"What do you mean, *don't look down?*" whimpered Susan. "How else can I see where to put my feet?"

"Okay. Can you reach my belt? Good. Just hold on to that. We'll take it one step at a time. I won't let go of one handhold until I've grabbed the next one."

Slowly the boy and the girl inched their way across the gorge. William, however, had not moved. He was sitting with one leg on each side of the immense log, and his whole body was shivering like the leaves of a quaking aspen.

"Come on, William," said Frigga gently. "Get up. You can do this. I will help you."

William just shook his head.

"Well, then, get up on my back, and I'll carry you. You're not too heavy."

"Noooo!"wailed William.

Hagen yelled something in an angry tone and flipped his hand toward William as if he were shooing a fly away from his supper.

"I think he's telling her to leave him," whispered Harold.

Frigga glared back across the gorge and shook her head. Then she laid her hand on William's head and spoke two strange words. William slumped to one side, but before he could fall off the log, Frigga picked up his small, unconscious body in her arms and stepped out to cross the gorge.

"Did you see that?" whispered Harold.

Susan just nodded. Scarcely breathing, she kept her eyes and her heart fixed on Frigga and the still form of her brother until the young woman stepped off the log and laid William at her feet.

"Is he okay?" she asked.

Frigga didn't answer. Instead, she touched the boy on the head and spoke few strange words. William sat up, rubbed his eyes, and looked around. "Where am I? How did I get here?"

"I'll explain," said Susan, "but I think we'd better talk as we walk. I don't think Hagen is too happy."

That evening as they sank to the ground in an exhausted heap, Susan sighed, "I hope we have something else besides those dry hard biscuits for supper. I bet they're a year old."

Frigga who had come up quietly behind her chuckled, "It's only been a few weeks since we made them, but they'd still be about the same in a year. We take them on long trips because they don't spoil. Anyway, your wish is about to be fulfilled. Come help me pull up those plants with the white flowers. We will boil the roots to go along with our supper."

"We call them Queen Anne's Lace," said Harold. "The roots

smell and taste like carrots, but they're very small."

"Ugh! Cooked carrots," said William. "I don't suppose you have any brown sugar and butter to put on them?"

"And there will be no chocolate cake for dessert either," laughed Susan.

"I don't know what chocolate cake is," said Frigga, "but maybe we can find some little round white things that grow under the ground to add to the carrots."

"Onions?" asked Harold. "Do you mean wild onions?"

Frigga didn't know the word *onions* either, but that is what she meant, and even William had to admit they helped the carrots. At least he didn't gag when he ate them as he sometimes did at home. They found patches of Queen Anne's Lace three more times in the next week of travel, and William complained a little less each time.

On the fourteenth evening of their trek, the group camped by a crystal-clear mountain lake. The next morning, the children were allowed to sleep late. Frigga stayed at the camp with them while the rest of the party headed off in different directions.

After the children had splashed cold water in their faces, Frigga said, "Let's see if we can't improve the taste of your breakfast biscuit. Susan and William, you pick the mint leaves over under that oak tree and drop them into the pot of water hanging over the fire. Harold, you come with me. See that old maple halfway up the hill? The one that looks as if it has been struck by lightning?"

Harold nodded.

"It's a honey tree. Let's go get some."

When they reached the tree, Frigga asked Harold place one knee on the ground while she used his other knee as a stepping stool. "I just needed a bit of a lift to reach the first branch," she said. "Now toss me the pot."

The bees were flying all around the boy and the Earth-Two

woman, but they did not seem at all angry when she reached into a hole in the tree and pulled out large piece of honeycomb dripping with sweetness.

"Why didn't they sting us?" asked Harold.

"I used their name; I told them to be calm," she said.

"And they listened?"

"Of course. Why not? Let's go have our breakfast." Back at the campfire, they crumbed their biscuits into large cups of mint tea sweetened with honey. "Much, much better," sighed William contentedly.

Harold tipped his cup up to get the last of his tea, and then looked hopefully, but unsuccessfully, for more biscuit crumbs in the bottom. "Can you do that with other animals, Frigga?"

"Do what?" asked William.

"She talked to the bees to calm them down so they wouldn't sting us."

"Yes, Harold. I can't make animals do everything I want, but when I speak their names, they won't harm me. Everybody here in Earth-Two can do that."

"Nobody in our Earth can do that," said Susan, "except in the movies."

"Could you calm a deer down enough so that you could stab it with a spear or something?" asked William. "Then we could have it for supper. I've been hungry most of the time since we left home."

"Not all of our people have that ability. I could do it, but I won't. We have flocks of sheep and goats and usually a few cows in our villages, and sometimes we eat those, but we don't normally use our power over the wild animals to kill them. It seems a bit unfair. If we were starving that would be different."

"I'm starving," muttered William.

Frigga laughed, "Growing boys are always starving. How about trout instead of venison? Come on. Let's see if we can catch some fish."

As Frigga rigged up hooks and lines for all of them, Susan caught grasshoppers for bait while the boys looked under a rotten log for grubs and worms.

As they stood by the lake a few minutes later, Susan asked, "Where did the rest of your group go, Frigga? Why are we here by ourselves with you?"

"They are searching for the exit vortex, which is supposed to be somewhere near here. It's almost time to send you back home. Won't that be nice?" Frigga smiled.

"Whoopee!" shouted William and Harold together.

"Yes," said Susan, "I will be glad to sleep in my own bed." Her mouth had said, "Yes," but to herself she thought, *Something's wrong. Frigga's heart was not in her smile.* Susan's earlier suspicions of Frigga, which had diminished under the woman's kindness in the past few days, began to grow again. Those suspicions were fully awakened by Frigga's next words.

"In order to send you back home, I will have to know exactly how you entered Earth-Two and how you planned to leave it."

The realization came like an explosion in Susan's mind: She doesn't know! She doesn't know how to open the doors between our worlds. These people need us to show them how to enter our Earth. But why?

CHAPTER 9—ANOTHER VORTEX

W hat words did you use to leave your Earth and enter mine?" asked Frigga?

"Coming here was more or less an accident," answered Susan. "We didn't really expect anything to happen. We were playing a game, just chanting a string of words, and then suddenly we were here."

Frigga, who was turned toward Susan, had her back to the boys. William opened his mouth to object to Susan's story, but Harold quickly put his finger to his lips.

"What were you chanting, Susan?" asked Frigga.

She spoke so quickly and eagerly that Susan was caught off guard and stumbled over her words, "I don't—I mean, we don't—"

"That's right, Frigga," interrupted Harold. "We can't tell you. It's a secret."

"Don't try that answer out on Hagen if he asks you!" snapped Frigga. "He's not nearly as patient as I am."

Frigga scarcely talked to them for the rest of the day, but she didn't leave them alone either. *She's not giving us any opportunity to talk by ourselves,* thought Susan. I bet she doesn't want to give us a chance to figure out how we're going to answer Hagen.

That evening, all of Frigga's companions except for Hagen returned one by one shaking their heads in disappointment. They ate supper in grumpy silence. Then the children were sent to go to sleep, but they were close enough for Frigga to hear them even if they whispered. Hagen returned a few minutes later. Lying beneath a giant oak tree, the children listened with growing anxiety to the conversation around the campfire.

Though they could understand none of the words, they could tell that Hagen was at first excited and then angry, apparently with Frigga. The conversation lasted long into the night. Before it ended, the children had fallen into a troubled sleep.

The next morning Frigga woke them early. "Time to go home," she said. "Come, eat your biscuit and tea. There's a little fish left over too. When you are done, I'll take you to the vortex. The others have already gone on ahead." Her voice was cheerful, and her lips smiled, but Susan looked at her eyes and saw something else. Was it sadness, or fear, or guilt?

After breakfast, Frigga led the children north along the lakeshore to a small stream that tumbled down from the surrounding hills. Turning away from the lake, they followed the stream into a deepening canyon. The way was difficult because there was no trail and the stream went all the way to the canyon walls in several places. It took them nearly two hours to reach the head of the canyon where they saw a small hill, shaped exactly like the two vortices with which they were familiar. Hagen and the rest of his band were already there.

"Here it is," said Frigga. "We have found a door back into your world. Now you can go home." Frigga led them to the top of the mound, shook hands with each of them, and stepped back. The four men and four women of Hagen's group formed a loose circle around the base of the hill. "It's okay. You may go now. Goodbye," she said.

Why didn't they ask us the passwords? wondered Susan. It seemed like a big deal to Frigga yesterday. What's going on?

Slowly Susan scanned the faces before her. Their eyes were blue and their hair various shades of blond, though none of the others could match the striking gold of Frigga's hair. With their muscular bodies and grim looks, they might have just stepped out of the book about the Vikings and their gods that she had read during the past term in school.

Those faces—were they the faces of friends or of foes? There was a tense eagerness about them. They reminded her of something, but what? Then she looked at Hagen, and she knew. His was the face of a cat waiting to pounce on a mouse. Suddenly she realized something else. She knew exactly what Frigga and Hagen and the rest of them wanted. She took the hands of her brother and Harold and commanded, "Follow my lead." Then she began to recite the chant they had used to enter Earth-Two the first time. Harold and William looked at her in surprise, but both had joined her by the third word.

When the chant was completed, the children remained standing in the center of the circle of expectant faces. For a few moments, no one moved. Then Hagen strode over to Frigga and began shouting at her and pointing toward the children. Frigga shook her head; Hagen shouted again, and again she shook her head. Finally, Hagen struck her hard, full across the face so that she fell to the ground. After a few moments, she tried to pick herself up, but before she reached a standing position, Hagen struck again. This time, Frigga crumpled at his feet and did not move.

"Frigga! Frigga!" screamed William. He rushed toward her side, but before he could reach her, rough hands had seized him and bound his arms behind his back. At the same, time Susan and Harold were captured and bound as well. At Hagen's command, two of the men picked up the limp Frigga; one of the women remained on guard at the vortex, and the rest returned down through the canyon to the camp.

That night, after they had been tied to a tree for the first time in over a week, Harold asked Susan to explain why she had led them in the entrance chant instead of simply saying the exit password, bahiH.

"I finally figured out what they wanted and why they dragged us along with them," she replied. "They don't know how to travel between the worlds. They hoped to use the exit near our home, but they couldn't after the landslide that covered the vortex...and Ulysses. If Ulysses hadn't been there, and if we hadn't happened along, I think they would have camped by the vortex and tried to leave Earth-Two by trial and error."

"I think you may be right, Susan," said Harold thoughtfully.

"When we stumbled into their path, they immediately saw that we were not from Earth-Two, and they assumed that we must know the passwords. That was Frigga's job, first to learn our language, and then to find out how we traveled between Earth-One and Earth-Two. If we had left Earth-Two this morning, they would have been right behind us. Maybe they were even planning to step up onto the hill and go right through with us."

"Well, so what if they did follow us?" asked William. "At least we would have been on our way home. Now what are we going to do?"

"This is the part I'm not very sure about, but I'll tell you what I think," replied Susan. "I think that they would have done something very bad in our world. I don't know what, but they can do things that nobody in Earth-One is able to do. I think that Ulysses was trying to prevent whatever harm they might be planning. If that's true, then Hagen might kill us once he learns what he needs to know. He wouldn't want us telling anyone who he is and what he can do. At any rate, I decided that it would be better for us to take our chances here than to help Hagen and his crew do something terrible to our world. I may be wrong, and you may disagree with me. If you do, I won't try to keep you from giving the password to Hagen."

The two boys were very quiet for several minutes. Finally Harold said, "I want to go home, but I'm willing to keep my mouth shut and to wait and see what happens."

"I will, too," sighed William, "but what do you think about

Frigga? Will she be okay?"

"I don't know, William. I hope so," said his sister. "I think she was trying to protect us. Even though she's been following Hagen, I think she really does care about us now."

William buried his head in his sister's lap and began to cry. "I want my mother. I want my mother."

* * **

That same evening less than two miles from where the children were tied up, Ulysses was rummaging through the packs on the donkey for the last of the food the Wilsons and Strutherses had brought with them. "I'm glad we haven't had to forage for something to eat," he said. "That would have slowed us down considerably. As it is, I've been able to spend more time on your training. You have done very well, Sam and Fred. We're about to find out if that training will pay off, but I hope you don't need to use it."

"Do you really think our children are nearby?" asked Fred?

"That is what I will try to discover later on tonight," replied Ulysses. "The exit vortex is only about three miles away, but I need to know where the rebels are located, assuming they are still here in Earth-Two. I don't want to blunder into their camp without some kind of plan. We won't light a fire tonight."

After a cold supper, Ulysses, the Wilsons, and the Strutherses spent an hour in prayer together. At the end of that time, Mr. Struthers flicked on his flashlight and read Psalm 50:15, "Call upon Me in the day of trouble; I shall rescue you, and you will honor Me." Then he prayed, "Father, this is certainly a day of trouble. Please rescue our children. If there is going to be a terrible battle tomorrow, we pray that You will soften the heart of at least one of the rebels and cause him to protect our children."

He paused, and all of them said together, "In Jesus' name, Amen." Then they lay down to sleep.

Shortly after midnight, the moon set, and Ulysses awoke. As silent as a shadow, and even less visible, he glided out of the camp into the slumbering forest.

CHAPTER 10—ESCAPE

Susan woke up with a start. A shadowy figure knelt over her, and she cried out in fear. William sat up with a puzzled grunt, followed by Harold.

"It's okay. I'm going to get you out of here," said a familiar voice.

"Oh, Frigga, are you all right?" asked William. "We didn't see you after we left the vortex."

"Yes, I'm fine. William. Nobody can hear us now because I've surrounded us with an air shield."

"A what?" asked Harold.

"An air shield. This kind blocks sound. I've no time to explain. When we start moving, I may be able to some muffle noises, but I can't cancel them out completely. You will have to be very quiet. Test every step before you put your weight down. I don't want any branches snapping."

"Where are we going?" asked Harold.

"I'm sending you to the nearest Earth-Two village. Just follow the stream that flows out of the lower end of the lake. You should reach it before night falls again."

"You're sending us?" asked William. "Aren't you coming with us?"

"No. Hagen is the best tracker I ever met—sometimes I think he could follow the path of a butterfly across a field of clover. He would have no trouble following us, and I don't want to face him and the rest of them in some narrow place along the stream. I think you will have a better chance of escaping if I stay here to fight."

"Fight? Why?" asked Susan.

"I finally realized that my parents were right. Hagen is a very bad man. If you don't tell him what he wants, I think he will kill you one at a time, hoping to make one of you talk. If you do tell him, he will probably kill you as soon as we reach your world."

"Won't he kill you for helping us escape?" asked William. He sounded as though he might cry, for he dearly loved Frigga.

"I'm not as strong as the men, but I know a lot more about fighting and defending myself than any of my companions do. I was being trained to be a ranger, but that's a story I don't have time to tell you now."

"What about wild animals?" asked Susan.

"I can't protect you from every danger, but if you see a saber-toothed cat say *shachal,* and it may leave you alone. No more questions now. We have to be going. I'll take you as far as the end of the lake before I come back here."

* * * *

Ulysses returned shortly before daybreak to brief the four parents. His face and voice were filled with concern as he spoke. "I found the rebels. One of the women was guarding the exit vortex. She is now tied up, gagged, and hidden where she won't be found if someone comes looking for her. The rest are camped by a lake over the ridge to the west of us, but I couldn't spot the children. That really bothers me. I'm afraid all we can do is climb to the top of the ridge, and then watch in secret until God makes our way clear."

Breakfast was a short, silent, somber affair. Leaving the donkey behind, the troubled parents followed Ulysses down into a deep, narrow valley and up the ascent of the western ridge. Ten feet short of the crest, they were jolted to a stop by an explosive sound coming from the far side of the hill. In two bounds, they were at the top looking down on a battlefield. They stood perhaps fifty feet above a narrow plain that stretched from the base of the ridge to the shore of a small lake. The plain was roughly twice as wide as a football field is long and was mostly covered with dry grass and scrub brush. A tall pine tree grew near the shore of the lake, and beside the pine stood a woman with hair like yellow gold.

Five of the rebels—three men and two women—were arranged in a large semicircle around the woman with the golden hair. Loud commands in the mother of all languages raised small boulders from the ground and sent them flying across the field. The brush and grass were ablaze, but the fire was not burning normally. Instead, the flames were dashing first toward one, then toward another of the combatants as they were being pushed about by invisible flows of air.

"What's going on? Why are they fighting?" asked Mrs. Wilson.

"No idea, but if anyone is likely to have befriended the children, it is that lone woman who is standing against the rest of them. I'm going to take them down."

"We can help," said Mr. Struthers. "Isn't that why you've been training us?"

"The two of you together could probably kill one of them, but you aren't well enough trained to disable them and leave them alive. There are only five, and I have the advantage of surprise. If I have a problem, which I don't expect, you are my backup plan. You are about to see what an Earth-Two ranger can do"

With that, he swooped down the steep face of the ridge as an eagle might dive toward an unsuspecting rabbit. One man stood almost directly beneath them. He went down with a quick hand chop. Two more rebels, one to the right and one to the left, fell almost as quickly. With their eyes fixed on the golden haired woman, they were not prepared to defend against an attack coming at them from the side.

"What did he do?" asked Mrs. Wilson. "I didn't see."

"He hit them in the back of the head with a small stone," said her husband. "Must have guided it using the Mother Tongue."

By this time, the rebels on both ends of the semicircle had seen him, and Ulysses had to deal with an alert enemy on either side. The woman at the lake turned to face the woman at Ulysses' left, so he spun to the right, but the man on that side did something unexpected. Instead of defending himself against Ulysses, he hurled a bolt of lightning at the tall pine. Even as the rebel fell before Ulysses' attack, the pine split with a mighty crack and toppled over, pinning the woman with the golden hair to the ground.

And so, in less than two minutes, all six rebels were down. While the parents scrambled down the slope of the hill, Ulysses ran to the fallen men and women and briefly touched the neck of each one. The parents could not make out the words that accompanied his touch, but even the half-heard syllables that reached their ears caused their throats to burn. Mr. Wilson and Mr. Struthers reached the golden-haired woman first, and by the time the others arrived, they had managed to pull her from beneath the crushing branches of the tree.

Her breathing was slow and ragged, but when her eyes finally focused on them, she made an effort to speak. "The children," she whispered hoarsely. "You must be their parents. They are in terrible danger. I cut them loose last night and sent them south around the lake to follow the stream down to the nearest village. I thought they might be able to make it before dark, but Hagen has followed them. I tried to keep him busy here with the rest, but I couldn't." Her eyes closed; her head slipped to one side, and she was still.

"Hagen is their leader," said Ulysses. "He's as mean as a grizzly bear. I'm going to try to save this one's life. You go after the children."

And so the parents began to run, not for their lives, but for the lives of their children.

* * * *

At that moment, the children were scrambling down a steep, rocky section of the streambed beside a waterfall. Below the falls, the stream widened out into a small pond. The upper end of the pond was clear and deep, but down the left side, a patch of tall reeds grew in a shallow backwater. William, who was better at climbing and jumping than his sister, reached the bottom first. He walked a ways along the right shore of the pond and then turned to watch Harold help Susan down the last and most difficult bit. Then he glanced back over the course of the creek above them and cried out, "Oh, no!"

"What's the matter?" asked Harold as he and Susan hopped from the last big rock to the gravelly shore of the pond.

"We're being followed. I only caught a glimpse of someone moving, but I think it was Hagen. What can we do?"

Harold trotted over to William's side, with Susan right after him. "Where?" he asked. "How far away was he?"

"Up there. Where we first started down the mountain," replied William.

"Okay," said Harold, looking at his watch. "It took us forty-five minutes to get this far, but I bet he'll make it in a lot less time than that. Wait here for a couple minutes."

Harold walked quickly to the far end of the pond where a series of rapids tumbled down a steep slope. He worked his way down the hill, dislodging stones at every opportunity. He grabbed several branches as if to steady himself, but he broke most of them and stripped the rest of their leaves. When he reached the end of the rapids, he stepped into the stream and climbed back up, being careful not to splash any water on the shore. When he reached William and Susan, he said, "Come on into the water and then pick up the biggest stone you can carry. Follow me to the other side."

William and Susan obeyed. The water was cold and nearly up to William's chin in the middle of the pond, but the shallow water among the reeds was somewhat warmer. Harold selected a tall reed for each of them and broke it off near the bottom and the top. "I read about this trick once in a book about Daniel Boone or somebody like that. Put the reed in your mouth and lie down in the reeds. You can breathe through your reed like a straw. Put the rock on your stomach to keep yourself from floating. Don't get up until I say it's okay. We'll stay here until Hagen has a chance to go past us, then we can look for a better place to hide."

Harold helped the others get settled. They insisted on grabbing their noses, which made it harder for them to hold on to their rocks. Harold didn't think the book had said anything about that, but he also found it necessary when he positioned himself between them. Harold lay as still as he could for what seemed like an hour or more, but when he cautiously raised his head to look at his watch it had only been five minutes. An eternal ten minutes later, he took a second cautious peek. Hagen was just disappearing over the slope at the end of the pond. Startled and frightened, Harold almost gasped aloud, but he stifled his cry and sank down again into his watery bed.

After a few more minutes of stillness, Harold sat up, looked around, and then poked William and Susan. They struggled together to their feet and stood for a moment, trembling from the cold and from fear. Their clothes were not only wet, but also muddy, so the children dipped themselves up and down in the water several times in an effort to wash them clean. Then Susan fell into the mud, and Harold had to help her up again. During this process, William watched with increasing horror as a broad, dark ribbon of muddy water snaked its way toward the rapids at the end of the lake. In silence he pointed at the ribbon, and then whispered, "What if Hagen—?"

"We've got to get out of here," said Susan. "Where can we go?"

"We can't go downstream," replied Harold, "and we can't climb the walls of this canyon without being seen. I remember seeing a crack or a crevice in the canyon a little way back. It's pretty steep, but maybe we can climb up there and hide for a few days. Whether or not Hagen sees the mud, he is going to realize pretty soon that we've given him the slip. It won't be long before he returns."

The children scrambled as quickly as they could back up the watercourse. They were out of breath and their hearts were pounding like heavy hammers in their chests by the time they reached the crevice. It was, indeed, quite steep, but William and Harold were sure they could climb it, and Susan was willing to try. As they stood at the bottom of the crack in the canyon wall, trying to figure out the best way up, a terrifying sound broke through their concentration and jerked them around.

It was the sound of Hagen laughing. He stood on the far side of the stream with his hands on his hips and his head flung back. His laughter held none of the warmth of a joke shared between friends. It was cold, cruel, and filled with murderous intent. Beside him stood two great cats with long, saber-like teeth protruding from either side of their snarling mouths. Slowly, Hagen raised one arm, pointed at the children, and uttered a loud command. In one bound, the tigers cleared the stream.

"*Shuchol!*" shouted Harold.

"No, *sheecal!*" shouted Susan.

"Maybe *sugar?*" cried William.

The great cats crouched to spring again.

In the next five seconds, several things happened that take much longer than five seconds to tell. As the cats were clearing the stream, the children's parents suddenly dashed out from behind a large boulder. They, too, had heard the laughter.

Mr. Struthers and Mr. Wilson quickly locked arms, spread

their feet apart for better balance, and with a loud cry pointed at the earth in front of Hagen. The ground on that side of the river rose in one long swell, like a wave of the sea approaching the beach. And like a wave of the sea, the swelling earth finally broke. A great crack opened up beneath the rebel; stones clattered down from the canyon wall above him, and when the dust had finally settled, Hagen could not be seen.

When the children turned their eyes from the rubble on the other side of the stream, they saw before them something equally amazing. Their mothers were standing beside the two saber-toothed tigers, scratching under the chins of the great beasts and murmuring calm, soothing sounds into their ears.

CHAPTER 11—HOME AGAIN

The hike back to Ulysses and the battle scene was tense. The parents and the children told their stories to each other, accompanied by occasional tears of joy. Beneath the happiness of their reunion, however, ran an undercurrent of anxiety as they worried about Frigga.

Frigga, as it turned out, was sitting with her back against a rock. Her left arm and right leg had both been broken by the falling tree, but by the time the Wilsons and Struthers arrived, Ulysses had rigged up a sling for her arm and a splint for her leg. Her face was pale, but she managed a smile when she saw the children. William ran over to her, knelt at her side, threw his arms around her neck, and cried, "Oh, Frigga! Oh, Frigga! I was afraid you were dead."

"Well, as you can see I am not. God has taken care of me and of you too, apparently. Odysseus—or Ulysses—says my arm and my leg will be as good as new in a couple of months." Frigga looked up at the other two children, who were standing before her. Then she continued, "Susan, you were quite right to be suspicious of me from the beginning, but in spite of that you were never nasty, and you always seemed to care about me. Thank you—all of you—for your clear witness for Christ. God finally used that to bring me to Himself."

Harold and Susan knelt beside William, and Susan gave Frigga a gentle hug. "I'm so glad," she said. "By the way, you called our friend Odysseus and Ulysses. Does he have two different names like some of the people in the Bible?"

"Apparently, but I don't know why. Maybe we can ask later."

As the children continued talking with Frigga, Mr. Wilson turned to Ulysses. He pointed at the five men and women tied to a nearby tree and said, "Aren't you afraid they will escape? Can't they break their bonds by using the mother of all languages? And how about the other woman you tied up last night? I didn't think about her before now."

"I'll have to fetch her before nightfall," replied Ulysses. "As for their using the Mother Tongue, the answer is *no*. I have destroyed their vocal cords. They will never speak again. The people of Earth-Two regard their language as one of God's most precious gifts, so destroying a person's ability to speak is one of the most serious punishments he can ever endure. Normally this is done only after a careful investigation and trial, but the Ruling Council of our people has given me the authority to execute this judgment in special circumstances. If these men and women were free to speak, I could never manage to take them back for a trial. That will take a few weeks to arrange, and I can't watch them every moment. If I ever left them, or even went to sleep, they would be able to free themselves. As it is, the council will now have to investigate to make sure that I have done the right thing."

"Is that what you were doing when you touched the rebels' necks after they were knocked out?" asked Mr. Wilson. "I felt something burning in my throat even though I couldn't really hear what you were saying."

"Yes, Fred. The words I used were so powerful that they were dangerous even to me. Only a few people know them, and they must be used with great care and knowledge."

Ulysses paused, looked up to mark the position of the sun, and said, "By the time we can get everything ready to leave, it will be dark. I suppose we might as well camp here for the night and go through the vortex tomorrow morning. Sam, will you please go for the donkey? Fred, can you make a travois for carrying Frigga, and perhaps the rest of you can find something for us all to eat. I need to fetch the woman I tied up by the vortex."

As the children headed off to fish in the lake, William whispered to Harold. "What is a travois?"

"It's something the Indians used for pulling a heavy load," he replied. "My fourth-grade teacher had us build a model Indian village. My job was to make a travois for a plastic horse. The Indians took two long poles and tied a blanket between them. The lower ends of the poles sat on the ground; the upper ends could be placed on an Indian's shoulders or hitched to his horse. I think Ulysses wants to use the donkey to pull the travois. That way Frigga will have a better ride than if she tried to sit on the donkey. When we come to the rough spots, our dads can pick up the end that's dragging on the ground."

"I wonder why Ulysses doesn't just make the rebels carry her?" mused Susan. "Maybe he doesn't trust them not to drop her *by accident*. I know *I* wouldn't want them to be carrying *me*."

The fishing expedition was only moderately successful, and the mothers were not as good as Frigga at finding edible plants, so supper was not very filling. No one complained, however, because they were all glad to be together, safe, and going home.

After supper as they sat relaxing around the campfire, William said, "Ulysses, why did the rebels call you Odysseus? Do you have two names?"

"Actually, I have three, though almost no one remembers my birth name any more. When I became a ranger, our training program was relatively new, and there weren't very many of us. Most rangers eventually settle down with a wife and family and go on missions as assigned by our Ruling Council. Our population centers are mostly in what you call Europe and Asia, so that's where most of our rangers are. I've always been a wanderer—never found a woman who wanted to wander with me—so they assigned me to all of North America.

"How can you cover such a vast area?" asked Susan.

"It has been many decades since some of our widely scattered settlements have seen me, but I go where I'm needed."

"What does that have to do with your names?" asked William.

"As I said, I've always been a wanderer. Odysseus is the name of an ancient Greek wanderer and warrior. One of my ranger friends started calling me that as a joke, and the name stuck. The ancient Romans called Odysseus, Ulysses. One of your presidents was named Ulysses, and the name doesn't seem too strange to Americans, so that's how I usually introduce myself."

"And your birth name?" asked William.

"My, you are persistent, aren't you?" chuckled Ulysses. "I haven't used that name in centuries, so I think I'll keep that bit of information to myself."

Early the next morning the party headed up into the hills toward the vortex. Harold was right about the donkey pulling the travois, which worked quite well. By nine o'clock they were at the vortex, and a few minutes later they had passed through it. Then Ulysses led them down the canyon toward a gravel forest service road that ran around the lake in Earth-One.

"If we may, I would like to stay with the prisoners at your homes for a while," said Ulysses. "I need to take them to Earth-Two through a vortex on the slopes of Mount Olympus in Greece. That vortex is very near to the capital city of my world, where our Ruling Council has its headquarters."

"How do you expect to get seven bound prisoners from here to Greece?" asked Mrs. Struthers.

"I plan to charter a small jet. We will take off from a private airstrip in America and land at another one in Greece. That way we will avoid passing through customs and airport security in both countries. I have friends in high places—very high places—who will clear our flight plans. It will take me a couple of weeks until everything is set up."

Mr. Wilson spoke first. "I'm sure we would all be glad to have you stay at our homes for as long as you like." The rest of the parents nodded.

"Why don't you fly them out of an Earth-Two airport?" asked William.

"Because if they don't even have cars," said Susan, "they for sure don't have planes. Can you imagine how many weeks it would take to walk to the Atlantic Ocean? Then I bet Ulysses would have to find a big sailing vessel that just happened to be going where he wanted."

"That's right, Susan. Our transportation is about like it was in your world before steamships and trains were invented. The people of our world still travel in ox carts and sailing ships, but Earth-Two rangers have developed a network of transportation contacts that enable us to move freely in your Earth.

"Sam and Fred, if I keep the prisoners off the road and out of sight, can you men hitchhike to the nearest town and arrange for transportation for all of us? Maybe you can call a friend who won't talk too much."

"Sure," said Mr. Struthers. "And it won't be necessary to call anyone to come for us. Don't ask me where in Earth-Two I thought I could use them, but for some reason I brought a credit card and my driver's license with me. I know where we are. There's a car rental not far away where I can get a couple of vans."

While Mr. Struthers and Mr. Wilson were off securing their transportation, the rest of the group sat down in a sheltered glen to rest. Susan perched on a rock beside Ulysses. "Isn't Mount Olympus where the ancient Greeks thought their gods lived?" she asked.

"Yes, it is. I suspect that some shepherds or farmers must have seen inhabitants of Earth-Two appearing and disappearing through the doors between our worlds, and that was the foundation for the legends."

The group continued talking for several minutes and then lapsed into silence as first one and then another dozed off. Ulysses woke them all an hour and a half later when he heard the vans stopping on the road. The men had brought burgers, fries, and sodas for lunch.

"Boy! This sure beats eating boiled roots!" said Harold. Everyone laughed in quick agreement. Later on that evening sitting at the long table in the Strutherses' home, the group had something even better to eat—baked ham, mashed potatoes, corn on the cob, and a fresh green salad. The rebels were fed in the basement of the Wilsons' house, where Ulysses had fashioned a temporary prison for them.

When supper was over, Ulysses said, "I have been thinking of the best way to wrap things up here. May I present my ideas?" He looked around the table to see the general nodding of heads.

"As I said, it will take a couple of weeks before I'm ready to take my prisoners away, but even after that I would like to impose on your kind hospitality from time to time. I would like to send three or four workmen to repair the exit from Earth-Two that was blocked by the landslide. Initially, they will need to camp near the exit vortex, but after the mound is uncovered, I think they would enjoy coming here each night as they finish restoring the valley."

"Of course," replied Mr. Struthers.

"I would also like to leave Frigga here for a few months. I have been very impressed by her, and I will speak on her behalf to the Ruling Council. She can give me vital information about the rest of her group still in Earth-Two. I gather that there were about three hundred of them who were waiting for the advance team to invade your Earth. Frigga is the best linguist of the whole group, and they were counting on her to break what they thought was a very difficult code to operate the vortices between our worlds. The reason I want to leave her here is so that she can begin to train you in the mother of all languages. The children know nothing and even you parents only know a few words and phrases. I want you all to learn to speak it well."

"Why?" asked Mrs. Struthers. "I thought your Ruling Council did not want people who knew the Mother Tongue to come here or people from Earth-One to go into your world."

"In general, that is true, Sharon, but there are exceptions. Earth-Two has always maintained carefully chosen representatives in your world. They must be people we can trust, people who will not use the Mother Tongue for evil. In your case, I see the hand of God at work in bringing you to Earth-Two. As I said, I don't know of any similar case in which people from your world just happened to discover how to enter mine. I do not believe in accidents. I believe in a sovereign God who does all things according to His own will."

"That is what we believe, too," said Mr. Struthers thoughtfully, and the rest of the parents nodded.

Ulysses continued, "I believe God has plans for you that involve Earth-Two, so with your permission, I want to leave Frigga here for a while to begin training you to speak the Mother Tongue. During the summer, she can spend more time with the children than will be possible after school starts. It will be soon enough to take her to Greece after that."

Turning to Frigga, he said, "I was very impressed with your performance yesterday morning. Who was your teacher?"

"Ajax and his wife took me into their home. He said I would make a good ranger. I lived with them for nearly two years before they died. Their ship sank in a storm far out at sea."

"Ajax was my friend, and a good ranger. I used to stop by their house from time to time to enjoy his wife's cooking. It's too bad that he died before he could complete the first phase of your training. If our Ruling Council approves—and I'm sure they will—I would like to see your training continued."

The next few days were busy ones. Many of those who had worried or prayed about the missing children had to come by to see for themselves that they were all right. Ulysses and Frigga were introduced as friends who had helped to find the children. The prisoners were kept out of sight until Ulysses finally took them to Greece. Frigga began teaching right away, but the constant coming and going meant that lessons were sporadic for almost a week. Then she began in earnest.

She taught the parents for an hour or two each night, but most of her energies were focused on the children. All day long, she worked with them, alternating lessons in grammar and vocabulary with physical exercise. "This is a lot harder than school," groaned Harold one afternoon. The three children had just collapsed after running a mile down the highway and back again.

"Yes, I expect it is, Harold," said Frigga, "but your ability to use the Mother Tongue well depends on more than knowing how to form sentences. Your bodies must also be in good shape. I am pushing you just as hard as you can bear it. I want you to be strong in mind and body so that you will be ready for whatever God may have in store for you. When you go back to school, we won't have as much time together, so I'm determined to make the most of the next few weeks."

Those weeks passed very quickly indeed. Mrs. Wilson drove them to school on the first day of class. They were eager to be early because they had not seen most of their school friends during the summer vacation. Their classmates knew that they had been missing for two weeks, and they all wanted to hear the details for themselves. A cluster of students quickly surrounded them and began asking questions. Since the children were not allowed to say anything about Earth-Two or the Mother Tongue, they had to leave out the most exciting parts of their time away, but they managed to give satisfactory answers anyway. They had lost their way and wandered far into the forest, but their parents, with the help of Frigga and Ulysses, had found them.

Everything was going quite well until Lenny Richards showed up. He was over the shock of being knocked down by Susan, and he had a few tough friends with him. "Well if it isn't Harriet back again! Hello, Harriet! I heard poor Harriet was lost this summer. Where were you? Couldn't you find your way home from across the street?"

Harold and William looked at each other. Then Harold said, "Susan, will you run ahead and call our friend to meet Lenny?"

Susan nodded and sped off toward the far end of the playground. Unlike most schools in large cities, the land for their old, country schoolhouse had been cleared from the surrounding forest. The farmers and ranchers who sent their children there had never seen a need for fencing it in.

Harold and William stepped to either side of Lenny and picked him up by the elbows. They followed Susan, carrying him as easily as if he had been a large doll won from a booth at the county fair. Some of the other students began to follow them, but stern glares from Harold and William stopped them. Lenny was kicking his feet and demanding to be let down, but the boys paid no attention.

Ten paces inside the forest they stopped. "Okay, Susan; bring him out," said Harold in a loud voice. Susan stepped from behind a large rock, and right behind her lumbered an immense, black bear. She walked over to face Lenny, and the bear moved up beside her. Placing her hand on the bear's head, she leaned over and whispered in his ear. Then she stepped to one side. The boys let go of Lenny and moved apart, leaving Lenny sprawled out on the ground in front of the bear. The bear took two steps forward, stood over the terrified bully, and proceeded to lick his face. Lenny fainted.

Lenny regained consciousness a few moments later when Susan poured a bottle of water on his face. The bear was gone, but Susan, William, and Harold were standing over him. Harold spoke sternly, "Lenny, I don't think it would be a good idea for you to mention this to anyone. You wouldn't want to meet our furry friend again, would you? I have one more thing to say. Why don't you drop those loser friends of yours and start coming to church?"

"And Lenny," added Susan softly, "if you do want to change, we'll be glad to help you." She looked kindly down at the frightened boy. Then, holding hands with her brother and her best friend on Earth, she began walking back toward school.

The Voyage

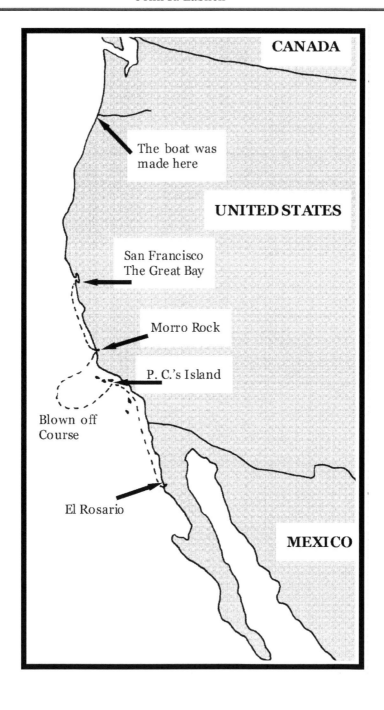

CANADA

The boat was
made here

UNITED STATES

San Francisco
The Great Bay

Morro Rock

P. C.'s Island

Blown off
Course

El Rosario

MEXICO

CHAPTER 1—SAN FRANCISCO

"D o I really have to go with you and Mom to San Francisco? I know it will be boring. You will go off to meetings all day, and I will have to follow Mom and a bunch of other ladies around as they shop at every store in the whole city. Can't I just stay with Susan and William? I'm sure their parents would let me sleep on the upper bunk in William's room."

"Yes, Harold. You have to go. It will be good for you to see a different part of the country, and besides we promised your great aunt Minnie that we would take you over to Oakland to see her while we were there. She has never met you, but she always sends you nice presents at Christmas and for your birthday. You will like her. I promise."

"Dad, I have another idea. May I invite Susan and William to go along with us? They will be on spring break, and Frigga will be gone, so they will be lonely too."

"Why won't Frigga be here?" asked Mr. Wilson. "I hadn't heard she was leaving. She was away in November for the trial of the Earth-Two rebels. Then last month she went to be tested to see if she could become a Ranger like Ulysses. I never heard if she passed, though."

"Yes, she did!" replied Harold. "Ulysses contacted her this afternoon with the good news. He wants her to come to Greece and enter Earth-Two through the vortex on Mount Olympus. She leaves on the day after tomorrow and will be gone for about a month. I think she will have to go back every year for a month or two of training."

Mrs. Wilson, Mrs. Struthers and the three children drove Frigga to the airport. She would fly to JFK airport in New York and from there catch an Olympic Airlines flight to Athens. They all went in and waited in line with Frigga at the ticket counter, but they had to say goodbye before she passed through the metal detector.

The children were all upset because they loved Frigga dearly, and she had never been gone so long before. Harold, as the oldest, was trying hard to pretend that his eyes were not leaking. Frigga stooped down, took his face between the palms of her hands and said, "In my world even the strongest and bravest men are not ashamed to cry. I don't know what went wrong in your country so that men are afraid to show others how they feel." She kissed him on the forehead, then turned to kiss Susan and William as well.

Finally, she handed Susan a small booklet. "This is for all three of you to share," she said. "I will be gone for a month and the booklet has thirty-one pages. Each page has a verse or two from God's word and a short explanation to go along with it. I have another copy of the same book. (I bought them yesterday when Mrs. Wilson took me into town to shop.) If you will read a page each day together and pray for me, I will do the same and pray for you. That way we will be together in spirit even if we can't see each other."

"Thank you," said Susan. "That sounds like a great idea. We'll start tomorrow morning." Harold and William nodded. Frigga turned, passed through the metal detector, picked up her purse on the other side of the x-ray machine, and with a wave was gone.

The next morning Harold, William and Susan went down to the bus stop in front of their house fifteen minutes early. Susan sat on the big, square rock they called "the castle," and opened the booklet Frigga had given her. The verse for the day was *Psalm 119:105*, "Your word is a lamp to my feet, And a light to my path."

"The primary way God guides us," she read, "is through His

word, the Bible. The lamps of ancient times did not send out their light very far. They only cast a circle of light around the feet. That is the reason the Psalmist says, 'Your word is a lamp to my feet.' If you carried such a lamp, it could only light your way one step at a time, but as you walked along it would gradually illumine your whole path.

"God's word does not show us our path ahead of time. It does not tell us where we will be next week or the week after, but if we walk one step at a time in the light of His word, we will be exactly where God wants us to be."

"I know where, I'm going to be the week after next," burst out William. "I'm going to be in San Francisco!"

"That's where you *think* you will be," replied his sister, "but only God knows for sure. Now don't interrupt. I'm not quite through with the page, and we still have to pray before the bus comes."

Susan moved her finger down the page to find her place. Then she continued, "How does God guide us by his word? One silly man thought he could discover God's will by opening the Bible at random and reading the first words he saw. He closed his eyes, turned a few pages, put his finger down and read, 'You fool! This very night your soul is required of you.' That frightened him, so he thought he should try again. Perhaps he would find a more comforting message. On his second attempt, his finger rested on the words 'Judas went away and hanged himself.' Now he was really scared, but he decided to try once more. This time his eyes rested on the words, 'Go and do the same.' The Bible does not guide us in that way, but by teaching us what is important and how we should live. When we obey the commands of God's word, He gives us light along our path."

Susan closed the book, and the children bowed their heads to pray for Frigga and for God to guide them through their day at school. When they opened their eyes again, the yellow bus was just coming around the corner. They jumped to their feet, grabbed their backpacks and stepped up to the side of the road.

"Waiting is so hard," said William as they slid into their seats. "I wish it were already the last day of school. I've never been anywhere on a plane, and San Francisco is going to be a lot of fun."

"Don't worry," laughed Harold. "It won't be long before we leave. My dad has a guidebook to the city. We can look at it every night and plan the things we want to do. That will help the days to pass." And it did.

On the Friday before spring break Mr. and Mrs. Wilson picked the children up from school. Mrs. Struthers was with them, and Mr. Struthers left work at noon so that he could meet them at the airport to say goodbye.

After they settled into their seats, Mr. Wilson pulled out a rectangular piece of cardboard with some lines and numbers on it. A piece of string with a large metal washer tied to the end was taped to one side. Mr. Wilson showed William how to hold the cardboard so that the string hung straight down through a mark in the center of the opposite side. When the plane took off the washer and string moved backwards. Susan watched to see how far the string moved while Harold timed the number of seconds they sped along the runway. Once they were up in the air, Mr. Wilson took out his calculator and did some figuring. After a few minutes he wrote down their speed at takeoff and the distance they had traveled down the runway. Then he gave the paper to a stewardess and asked her to take it to the captain. The children didn't understand the math, but they were impressed when the captain came back into the cabin to congratulate them on the accuracy of their results.[1]

---

[1] If you want to see how Mr. Wilson performed this experiment look in Appendix 1 at the end of the story. My son and I did it once on a cross-country flight and obtained surprisingly accurate results. The

"Wow! That's pretty cool," said a boy sitting across the aisle. "I've been in airplanes lots of times, and I've never seen the captain come back to talk to anybody before."

It was late by the time they reached their hotel suite, but the children were too excited to go to bed right away. "Dad and Mom, watch," said Harold. "We want to show you something. We learned how to do it all on our own after Frigga left."

William sat down on the floor by the sliding glass door that led to the balcony. Harold and Susan stood side by side holding hands on the opposite side of the room. They looked straight at William and said in the Mother Tongue, "William rise." William remained in a sitting position, but his body rose straight up in the air. Then in the same language they called out, "William come." And he came, floating across the carpet until he bumped into Harold and Susan and knocked them over. Then he fell right on top of them.

Mrs. Wilson laughed, "That's pretty good, but you need to work on the landings. I bet you and Susan are exhausted by now, but how are we going to get William tired enough to go to bed? Well, tired or not you'd better head off. Tomorrow will be a big day for all of you."

If Mrs. Wilson had known just how big a day it would be, she would never have allowed them to leave the hotel.

---

captain sent us a note, but he did not come back to talk to us.

CHAPTER 2—TRAPPED

The next morning Mr. and Mrs. Wilson took the children to breakfast and then down to the marina where a number of large party boats were docked. Mr. Wilson's boss had planned an overnight trip for company executives and some of their business contacts. Mr. Wilson called it a "cruise and booze" trip. After he had become a Christian two years earlier, he began to see how destructive alcohol was in his life, so he stopped drinking. He didn't want to go on the trip, but his boss insisted, so Mr. Wilson asked his wife to go along—"for protection," he said.

As the boat pulled away from the dock, Mrs. Wilson called out, "Don't forget to be in the hotel before dark. You can go to the early church service tomorrow morning and then meet us here when we come back at noon. Good-bye. God be with you."

The children waved and replied in chorus, "And with you, too." That had become their standard farewell a few months ago after Harold had learned at school that "good-bye" was a contraction of "God be with you."

Mrs. Wilson turned away from the railing to scan the deck for her husband. He was already deep in conversation with some other men near the bow of the boat. It looked like business, so she decided not to interrupt. The lady standing next to her caught her eye and spoke up, "Hello. My name is Gloria. I don't mean to be rude, but are those your children? Are you leaving them all alone overnight in a strange city?"

"Well, one of them is mine. The older boy. The other two are neighbors. Oh, by the way, my name is Wilma. And yes, they will be alone, but I'm not worried. I used to fret about Harold whenever he was out of my sight, but that was before last summer."

"What happened last summer?" asked Gloria.

"It's a long story," replied Mrs. Wilson, "but they have been receiving a very special kind of survival training under a very special teacher. This past winter she decided it was time to put their skills to the test. Our houses back up against a state-designated wilderness area. No roads or electric lines or anything goes through it. The day after Christmas their trainer—Frigga is her name—set them down at the far side of the wilderness and told them to walk home. That is forty miles as the crow flies. They knew the general shape of the land from hiking in it all summer, but she sent them out with no food, no knife, no compass and no map. The first night it snowed. The second night there was freezing rain. Fred and I were worried sick, and so were the parents of the other children, but not Frigga. On the fifth day they showed up, healthy and happy. Not only that, but they brought out with them an experienced hiker who had fallen and broken his leg. (Mrs. Wilson decided not to mention that Susan had called on a bear to carry the injured hiker.)

Gloria breathed out a quiet "Oh" of astonishment. Then both women turned to watch the children walking up the ramp from the dock to the level of the street.

They sat down on a bench overlooking the marina to read from the devotional booklet Frigga had given them. The verse for the day was Psalm 20:7, "Some trust in chariots and some in horses, but we trust in the name of the LORD our God (Psalm 20:7, ESV).

"How should we apply that verse to our own lives?" asked William. "We don't have any horses or chariots—only the donkey back home."

"I think," replied Susan, "we should not be too sure that we can take care of ourselves. Frigga has taught us so much, and we might be in danger of trusting in everything we have learned. We should trust in God, not in ourselves."

After they had prayed, the children set out to explore the city. They had a wonderful day. They began by walking east as close to the waterfront as they could. It was about two miles to Fisherman's Warf where they bought hot dogs from a street vendor. Then they spent a couple of hours in *Ripley's Believe It or Not*. When they came out, Harold's opinion was, "Mostly not."

The *Wax Museum* was next door, so they went in there. Susan liked the beautiful costumes of the rich and famous; the boys spent most of their time looking at exhibits of the bad and the ugly. From there they walked up Mason Street to catch the cable car to Chinatown. The boys wanted to hang on to the special poles on the outside of the car, but Susan insisted they ride inside with her.

Chinatown was even more fascinating than the museums. It was almost like entering another world. Many of the signs were in Chinese characters, and in the shops used by the locals the children were immersed in a buzz of foreign sounds and smells. They had Chinese fortune cookies and an ice cream cone for a snack and then looked for souvenirs at the Far East Trade Center.

Susan bought a Chinese fan. The stiff paper of the fan was decorated with beautiful birds, and the bamboo frame folded up small enough to fit into her purse. William was fascinated by Chinese "handcuffs"—really not handcuffs at all but a small tube woven from something like palm fronds or bamboo leaves. His fingers slid easily into the two open ends of the tube, but when he tried to pull them out again, the tube tightened around his fingers and would not let go. Harold helped him out of the contraption the first time, but after that he figured it out for himself. Harold's prize find was a Chinese puzzle box. In order to open the box, he had to slide three secret panels and push a hidden button.

The sun was low on the horizon as the children wandered aimlessly through the streets and alleys of Chinatown. Harold and William were playing with their new Chinese toys. Susan was walking ahead of them and thinking that it was just about time to head back to the hotel.

She stopped so suddenly that the boys bumped into her from behind. "Shhh!" she whispered. "Look down that alley." A tall woman in jeans and a black sweatshirt was holding the wrist of a girl about Susan's age. The girl was shaking her head and trying to pull away. As the children watched, the woman yanked the girl off balance and dragged her through an open door. The door banged shut.

"I don't like the looks of that," said Susan.

"Neither do I," answered Harold. "I don't think that woman is her mother."

The children walked slowly and cautiously down the alley. Even before they reached the door, they could hear a child crying out, "Help! Help! Somebody help me."

"Shut up, brat," snarled a woman's voice. "There, that'll take care of you, I reckon." Then an inner door slammed; then there was silence.

"What should we do?" asked William. "Should we call the police?"

"I don't know," replied Susan. "I think we should ask God for wisdom. Remember our verse from this morning? God wants us to trust Him, not our own bright ideas. Harold will you please pray for us?"

Harold bowed his head. "Dear Lord, we do not want to do anything on our own. We are afraid that something very bad is happening to that girl. We trust you to guide us. In Jesus name, Amen."

On the very last word of the prayer, the children heard a loud moan and a series of muffled sobs from beyond the door. "Let's just try the door knob and see if it's unlocked," said Harold. To his surprise the knob turned, and the door swung in easily with just a light push.

The room was dark except for the last fading rays of daylight coming in through the open door. It appeared to be the back entrance and storage area for some kind of shop. Boxes were stacked in neat piles, but the floor was littered with bits of cardboard, bubble wrap and packing tape. In the far left-hand corner lay a quivering bundle of human flesh. The girl they had seen was bound hand and foot and her mouth was covered with duct tape.

Susan rushed over, knelt beside the trembling girl, and whispered, "Don't make any noise. We'll get you out of here." She carefully pulled the tape from the girl's mouth while William and Harold freed her hands and feet.

The four children had just gotten to their feet when they heard voices from beyond the inner door of the storeroom. A woman was saying, "This girl is the last one. You asked for twenty-five children. I've brought you twenty-five children. Now I want to be paid."

"Oh, you will be. You're going to get exactly what you deserve." The laugh that followed was cold, cruel, and terrifyingly familiar.

"Hagen!" whispered William. "I thought he was dead!"

"So did I," answered Susan, "but don't you remember how worried Ulysses was when he couldn't find Hagen's body? I bet he crawled out of the rock slide, followed us to the vortex, and heard us use the password. What are we going to do, Harold?"

Before Harold could answer, the inner door burst open, a light came on, and the children found themselves facing their most dreaded enemy. Hagen spoke two words in the Mother

Tongue, and all four children slumped to the floor, unconscious.

CHAPTER 3—INTO EARTH-TWO

Harold woke up one inch at a time, starting with his head. It hurt. He started to cry out in pain, but his mouth wouldn't open. Then he noticed that he could not move his arms or his hands; next that many sharp points were digging into his back, and finally that he was wet and cold from his chest all the way down to his toes. With that his eyes popped open.

The moon was nearly full, but even so it took a minute or two for him to figure out where he was. Susan, William and he were tied with steel cables to wooden pilings under a pier; Susan and William were not moving. The pain in his back came from barnacles and mussels growing on the pilings. His mouth was covered with duct tape. Then he remembered Hagen. Hagen! He wanted them to drown! The tide was coming in, and within an hour water would be over their heads. Harold thought of Tiger Lilly and wondered briefly if Peter Pan would come flying to their rescue.

Then panic set in. What good were all the wonderful lessons Frigga had taught them? He could not use the Mother Tongue because he could not speak at all. And even with the Mother Tongue he didn't have enough strength to break the steel cable that bound him to the pier. He struggled to get free, but that only made the cable bite more deeply into his bare arms. At last he began to cry.

In the midst of his tears, he thought he could hear Susan's voice speaking in his mind. It seemed so real that he looked to see if she had gotten free, but both she and William were still unconscious. He shut his eyes, and the voice was still there. Susan was reciting the verse she had read that morning, "Some trust in chariots and some in horses, But we trust in the name of the LORD our God." Susan was right. Their knowledge of the Mother Tongue could not save them. Only God could rescue them.

Harold began to pray, "Lord, I cannot do anything to help us. Please rescue us. Please keep us from drowning. I trust in you and not in myself. In Jesus' name. Amen." Harold lifted his head and looked around. Nothing had changed, but he was not afraid any more.

The night was still, broken only by the gentle sound of waves lapping against the pilings or breaking on the shore. The night was still, but as Harold listened, the stillness was broken by a man's voice. His words were slurred and faint, but gradually they grew louder. "I'm no good to anybody. Just a stupid, worthless drunk. I might as well be dead. Lord, do you hear me? I'm gonna drown myself. That's what I'll do. I'm gonna walk right out into this bay here until the water is over my head, and then I'll just die."

Harold and the man saw each other at the same instant. "Hey! What's this? A kid tied to one of the pilings? No, there are three of them." The cold water and the sight of the children must have shaken the man from his drunken confusion. He floundered quickly through the deepening water and tore the tape first from Harold's mouth and then from the mouths of Susan and William. That woke them up! "Don't worry," he said. "I'm a locksmith. My name's Joe. I have a cable-cutter in my van. I'll be right back."

And he was. William had to be carried ashore because he was too stiff and sore to swim, but Susan and Harold were tall enough to touch bottom, so they made it in on their own. Joe led them to his van, wrapped them in a couple of blankets and then picked up some sandwiches and hot chocolate at an all-night gas station. "Now," he said, "What's up? Who was trying to drown you, and why? Where are your parents? I suppose I should call the police."

"No, not the local police," replied Harold. "Hagen, the man who tried to kill us, has some very special abilities. They could never catch him. We have to contact Ulysses, who is probably in Greece. I guess you could call him an international policeman. If our parents were here, they might try to capture him, but my mom and dad are on a cruise until noon tomorrow, or is it today? Susan's and William's parents are back home. So the three of us will have to decide what to do."

"What do you mean, the three of you? I've already decided. I'm going to call the police. Special abilities, my foot. What could this Hagen guy do in the face of San Francisco's SWAT team?"

"Let's put him in an air shield while we talk," said William.

"Good idea, William," replied Susan.

The children held hands, looked intently at Joe and said a few words in a foreign language. The first thing Joe noticed was that he could no longer hear the children talking, even though their lips were moving. He stretched out his hand and it ran into an invisible wall. The wall was soft, but he could not force his way through it, and it went completely around him. For a moment he was frightened; then he became angry, and finally he sat in silent amazement watching the children as they discussed what they should do.

Outside the air shield, William was saying, "I just want to go back to the hotel. I'm so cold and tired."

"I am too," replied his sister, "but we can't leave that girl in Hagen's clutches. Who knows what will happen to her? I say we should go back and see if she is still there. And what about the other children? The woman said that the girl was the last of twenty-five. What do you think, Harold?"

"I think we need God's guidance. Susan, do you still have the devotional book Frigga gave you? Why don't we read today's page?"

"Yes. It's a little damp, but not soggy. I guess my purse must have been floating most of the time." Susan opened the booklet carefully and read the verse at the top of the appropriate page: 'Deliver those who are being taken away to death, And those who are staggering to slaughter, Oh hold them back' (Proverbs 24:11)."

"Wow! Talk about a quick answer from God," exclaimed Harold. "Do you remember when our pastor spoke on that verse last January? He was talking about protecting the lives of unborn babies. That girl isn't a baby, but she is in danger. We know the police can't defeat Hagen, but we might be able to help, so we should go."

William reluctantly nodded his head. After a brief planning session, they turned again toward Joe and spoke a few words. The air shield collapsed, and Susan said, "Joe, there is another girl, and maybe several other children, who are in great danger. We believe God wants us to try to help her. You have seen that we have some special abilities of our own. If you are willing to help us, we will give you a job to do. If not, we will have to make sure you stay here for a while. We need you. Are you in?"

"A little while ago," answered Joe, "I wanted to die because I thought no one needed me. If you think I can help, well, sure, I'm in."

Ten minutes later the little group was creeping down the alley. When they reached the door, it proved to be locked, but Joe opened it in a few seconds without making any noise. They peered cautiously inside as Joe shone his flashlight from one end of the room to the other. The girl they had come to rescue was nowhere to be seen, but in the far left-hand corner lay a woman, bound hand and foot with the all-too-familiar strip of duct tape across her mouth. She was the same woman they had seen kidnapping the girl. As soon as the duct tape was removed, she cried, "Get me out of here before he comes back. He's going to kill me. That's what he said."

"Who's going to kill you, miss?" asked Joe.

"Hagen, I bet," said Harold. Then turning to the woman he said, "Do you remember us?" The woman gasped with the shock of recognition, and Harold continued. "God rescued us from drowning. With His help we will see you to safety as well. Now, where is the girl?"

"Hagen took her downstairs. He takes them all downstairs, then they just disappear. I can't understand it because there is nothing down there except a dirt floor with a mound in the middle of it. When he comes back, it's not from the basement but from somewhere else."

"We know how he disappears," said Harold, "but what is he planning to do with the children? Do you know?"

"I didn't know for sure until tonight," replied the woman. "After he took you away, he came back and said I was going to get what was coming to me. Then he tied me up. I think he is planning some special kind of torture for me. Before he carried the girl downstairs, he took a few minutes to gloat, probably because he was so pleased at the thought of you three drowning. He plans to send the children I captured on a boat to Baja California. I think he is going to drive down and meet them near El Rosario in a couple of weeks. Then he will sell the children for $2,000 each to an international slave trader. Now, let me out of here. I've got to be gone before he gets back."

"Wait a minute," said Susan. If you leave on your own, Hagen may find you. We can send you someplace safe. William, Harold, are you with me?" Both boys nodded solemnly. "We three are going downstairs, where we will disappear. Joe, please take this lady to our hotel. Here is the key card for our suite. Harold's parents should show up shortly after noon. (They can protect you, Miss, even against Hagen.) They will be worried because they expect us to meet them at the marina. Tell them everything that has happened. We may be able to come back to the hotel ourselves, but if not, we will try to sneak on board the boat. In that case, they can look for us at the vortex near El Rosario."

"There is a third possibility," remarked Joe. "You may be dead."

"Yes, we know that," answered William. "I'm scared, but all three of us believe this is the right thing to do. God is able to protect us, and I hope that He will, but if not—well, we all know Jesus as our Savior. If we die, we are sure that we will be with Him."

With that the children turned and headed downstairs. Joe wanted to stay and watch them disappear, but the frightened woman dragged him out the door and down the alley toward the van.

CHAPTER 4—SETTING THE CAPTIVE FREE

As soon as Joe and the woman slid into their seats in his van, she said, "Let's get out of here. You can go to the hotel if you want and wait for the parents of those kids, but I'm going to leave on the first bus headed east. Take me to the bus station; I don't want to be in the same state as Hagen, and I don't ever want to see the parents of those kids. You can be sure they will call the cops if their kids don't show up, and they might anyway."

For a moment, Joe just looked at her. "Those kids saved your life at the risk of their own. Now they may die trying to rescue a girl they don't even know. What kind of a human being are you anyway?" He snorted in disgust, turned the key and drove the woman to the station. As he backed out of the parking lot, he saw her racing for a bus labeled "Chicago Express." Then he headed for the hotel, his heart filled with concern for the children he had rescued from certain death.

* * * *

As Joe and the woman were heading toward the bus station, William, Susan and Harold stood on a slight mound of earth in a damp basement. Harold reached out to hold hands with the younger children and found that Susan's hand was shaking. They prayed together; then together they spoke a single word in the Mother Tongue. Seconds later they were standing inside the ancient forests of Earth-Two. The moon was bright, so it was easy to see that they stood on a small hill in the middle of a clearing surrounded by large pines and sequoias. Harold swept around the circle with Joe's flashlight. Almost immediately they spotted the kidnapped girl tied to one of the trees.

"Who are you?" she asked Susan as the boys began to untie

her. "That horrible man, Hagen, was laughing about killing you. He wanted to go and watch your bodies reappear as the tide went down. That's why he left me here. He said he would come back in the morning to take me down to the boat. Where are we anyway?"

"I'm Susan Struthers. This is my brother William, and the other boy is Harold Wilson. Obviously we are not dead. God sent someone to rescue us, and we have come for you. We can't tell you where we are, but we can take you back to San Francisco. Do you remember which direction Hagen took when he left here? Oh yes, and what is your name?"

"I'm Andrea Jones, and Hagen went that way." Andrea pointed a little to the right of the vortex mound. Susan helped her to her feet and held her hand while the boys walked ahead of them in the direction Hagen had taken.

"You're not going to follow him are you?" cried Andrea. "That's crazy."

"No, that is the safest direction we can go," replied Susan. "This mound is the entrance from our world to this place. He is headed for the nearest exit. When he returns he will simply appear on this mound, but until he comes back and finds you gone, he will have no reason to watch the exit. All three of us are pretty good trackers, but William is the best. With the full moon and the flashlight he shouldn't have any trouble following Hagen's trail, especially since he must have gone that way many times in the recent past."

As they walked, Andrea told them her story. Her mother and father were divorced. Because her mother was on drugs, the court had given her into the custody of her father, whom she dearly loved. One day, however, her mother picked her up after school and took her away. They lived for a while in Reno, Nevada, but for the last few months they had been in Las Vegas.

As Andrea described her horrible life with her mother, Susan felt hot tears running down her cheeks. She was glad it was too dark for anyone else to notice. At last, Andrea ran away from her mother. Catching rides with various strangers, she finally managed to get to San Francisco where she hoped to find her father. He wasn't living at their old apartment, however, and no one there seemed to know where he had gone.

By the time she finished her tale, the children had found the exit vortex. William, Susan and Harold held hands around Andrea and prepared to speak the word in the Mother Tongue that would take them back to San Francisco. Suddenly, Harold spoke up. "I've been thinking. What about the other twenty-four children? If we go back through the vortex with Andrea, we won't be able to do anything for them. I wonder if we can send her through without going ourselves?"

"How can we do that?" asked Susan.

"This may not work, but how about trying this. We will put her on the center of the mound, but we will stand off the mound on three sides. Then on the count of three we can say the exit password together. That may open the gate for her, but not for us. Are you willing to try it? We haven't much time to decide because it is beginning to get light, and Hagen may be back soon."

"I don't know what to think," replied Susan. "Your idea might work, but what if Hagen catches us here? And even if he doesn't, what can we do?"

"We could just hide and watch and listen," said William. "We might find out something that would be useful. Why don't you pray for us, Susan? Ask God what we should do."

Susan and the rest of the children bowed their heads. Her voice was a little shaky at first, but it grew stronger as she prayed: "Dear Father in heaven, You are greater and wiser than our parents back on our earth. They are not here, but You are everywhere. We cannot ask them what to do, so we are coming to You with our question. Proverbs 2:6 says, "For the Lord gives wisdom; from His mouth come knowledge and understanding." So we are coming to you for wisdom. What should we do? Should we go with Andrea or stay here? In Jesus' name, Amen."

Susan opened her eyes and looked at William. After a few moments he nodded his head. "Okay. Let's try it, Harold," she said.

They placed Andrea at the center of the mound, gave her instructions on finding Harold's parents and with a word sent her from Earth-Two back into San Francisco.

As Andrea stood on top of the mound, the forest and her three new friends began to spin around her. The sight made her dizzy, so she fell to her knees and closed her eyes. When the world stopped moving, she opened them. Seeing absolutely nothing, she shut them for a few seconds, then opened them again. Still there was nothing. Had she become blind?

With her heart pounding in her throat, she began to crawl. She felt her way down a small mound of earth, across a short, flat space and right up to cold, stone wall. Suddenly she realized the truth. She was in the dark basement of an old house. Slowly she stood up and began groping along the wall, searching for a door or a light switch.

The door came first. It was big, heavy and stuck, but when she finally pulled it open, a glimmer of light illuminated concrete steps that led to large, metal bulkhead doors. Fortunately, they were not locked, only secured on the inside by a sliding bolt. Andrea pushed the bolt to one side, cautiously raised the left-hand door, stepped out, and looked around.

She seemed to be in a small park. The building from which she had escaped might have been some kind of historical site, but she didn't stop to investigate. Instead she walked straight up to the first person she saw and asked directions to the hotel where the Wilsons were staying.

Since she had no money, she had to walk all of the way. It took her over two hours, so she was very tired and very hungry when she arrived. Her clothes were ragged and dirty and her hair uncombed, so it is no wonder that doorman at the hotel stopped her before she entered.

"Where are you going, miss? I don't remember seeing you here before."

Andrea looked down at the man's shiny, black shoes. There was a lump in her throat and fear in her heart. For a few moments she considered running away. Then she looked up at his face. He was old and very serious, but his eyes seemed kind. At last she answered in a very small voice, "Please, sir, I want to visit the Wilsons staying in room 508. I met their son and two of his friends who told me to come here."

The doorman pushed open the heavy glass doors and personally escorted her to the elevator. When it came, he pushed the button for the fifth floor, and said, "When you get off turn right. 508 is just four doors down. Goodbye, miss. Have a nice visit."

Outside the Wilson's room, Andrea stopped, took a deep breath and knocked. A few moments later the door opened and Andrea found herself looking up into the face she loved best in all the world. "Daddy," she cried, "What are you doing here?"

"Andrea, Andrea, is it really you? I thought I would never see you again. I missed you so much, and I felt so miserable that last night I almost took my own life." Joe, her father, picked her up, kissed her, carried her into the room, and shut the door.

Joe ordered up breakfast for Andrea from room service, and for the next hour he and Andrea traded stories. Joe told about saving Harold, Susan, and William from drowning. Andrea explained how these same three children had rescued her. Then she curled up in her father's lap and slept for perhaps forty-five minutes. She awoke with a scream.

"What's the matter, honey?" her father asked.

"I was having a dream about that horrible man, Hagen. Daddy, I'm scared. Let's just leave. Please take me someplace far away, right now."

"You know I can't do that, Andrea. I have to stay here to tell Harold's parents what has happened. If we leave now, they won't even know where to start looking. If the children don't come back, their parents will not go to meet them at El Rosario. Harold, Susan, and William saved your life. We can't desert them."

"But, Daddy, what if Hagen finds us? What if you take Mr. and Mrs. Wilson to the place where I was captured and Hagen is there? I think he could kill you with just a look or a word. I don't want to lose you again. Can't you write a letter explaining everything to the Wilsons and leave it where they will see it? Please, Daddy."

Joe looked down at his frightened daughter for several seconds. Finally he sighed and said, "Okay." He set Andrea down beside him on the couch, and with suggestions from her he began to write. The letter took quite a while to compose and filled both sides of a large sheet of hotel stationery.

When he had finished, Joe laid the letter on a bed near the open balcony door. Then, hand in hand, father and daughter left the room. As the door closed behind them, they did not see the powerful gust of wind that blew the letter from the bed and over the railing of the balcony. Neither did they recognize Mr. and Mrs. Wilson, who passed them as they walked out of the lobby of the hotel.

CHAPTER 5—SETTING SAIL

As Joe and Andrea left the hotel, Susan, William and Harold were being wakened from a short, but sound sleep. After Andrea had disappeared from Earth-Two, the children used every trick Frigga had taught them in order to hide from Hagen.

They walked backwards along their path from the entrance to the exit vortex. Whenever they could, they stepped exactly in the footprints they had made earlier that morning, and they carefully erased any extra tracks they accidentally made. That way Hagen would think they had gone straight to the exit vortex and back into San Francisco. When they had gone about three hundred yards, they stopped and Susan did two things.

First, she called in a flock of crows and left them to watch the trail. She knew that they would naturally sound an alarm if Hagen came that way. Second, she summoned a bear to walk behind them as they turned off the trail. The bear's waddling tracks easily covered their passage through the brush back to within one hundred yards of the exit vortex.

It was nearly nine o'clock when they stopped for a drink at a clear spring and then crawled under an immense pine tree. Beneath the tree there was plenty of room for them to sit up, but its outer branches drooped all the way to the ground, so they were completely hidden. Susan pulled two leftover sandwiches from her purse for their breakfast, after which the children collapsed into an exhausted and dreamless sleep.

Two hours later the crows began to caw. William, who was the lightest sleeper, was the only one who heard them. It took him several seconds to remember where he was. Then he crawled over to Harold and whispered, "Hagen," and together they gently roused Susan.

With wildly beating hearts the children sat and listened. Four or five minutes after the crows sounded the alarm, Hagen began shouting in the vicinity of the exit vortex. William turned to Harold, looking puzzled. "I can hear him well enough, but I don't know what he is saying."

Harold leaned over and whispered, "Frigga didn't teach us those words. I think he is swearing."

After a minute or two the shouting stopped, only to be replaced by a sound that caused the children to tremble with fear. Hagen was coming. They could hear him crashing through the brush, breaking a new trail and heading straight toward their hiding place. As they held their breath, he stomped right up to their tree, circled around it to the right, and headed down toward the bay.

"Whew, that was close," sighed William. "I could even see his feet. If he hadn't been so angry, he might have noticed where we crawled in under the branches. God certainly took care of us that time. What do we do now?"

"We wait a few minutes, and then follow him," replied Harold.

Hagen's trail led down over the steepest part of the hill. The children had no trouble following it, and they were not much afraid that he would come back that way. It was obviously not his normal path for walking from the bay back up to the exit vortex. As they neared the water, they went more slowly and cautiously. At the edge of the last steep incline above the water they stopped and stared.

Below them, anchored in the bay, lay a wooden sailboat. Two men were rowing a dinghy from the sailboat to the shore, where Hagen stood waiting. Fortunately his back was turned toward the children.

Susan made signs to her brother and Harold to stay and watch while she slipped down over the brow of the hill. Frigga had worked hard with Susan to develop her natural ability to hide and to move quietly through the forest. Now that training was paying off. As silently as a shadow, Susan slipped from rock to tree to bush. Most of the time even Harold and William could not see her, and they prayed that the men below them would not. She stopped only a short stone's throw from Hagen. A cluster of red-barked madrona trees sheltered her from his view as the two men in the dinghy stepped ashore.

"Hi, Boss. What's up?" asked the taller of the men. "Do you have more cargo for us?"

"He's speaking English with an American accent," thought Susan. "That means he is not from Earth-Two."

"No! Shut your foolish mouth. I ask the questions; you give the answers. I give orders; you do what I say. Have you seen three children wandering about on the shore or any men or women?"

"No, Boss."

"Well, there has been a change of plans. There won't be any more captives, and I'm not coming back here. If you ever want to see your world again, meet me along with the boat off El Rosario. I want you to leave immediately."

"Okay, Boss, but we can't weigh anchor for another three hours. The tide is still coming in. We get seven times as much water rushing through the Golden Gate as flows out the mouth of the Mississippi River. No sailboat can make headway against that kind of current, so we have to go out with the tide."

Hagen said nothing in reply. He glared at the men for a few seconds, then turned on his heel and began stalking away. The men stood still and watched as his back disappeared among the tall evergreens. Finally, the one who had been silent spoke.

"He's a strange one, Pete, and scary to boot. I bet the reason he isn't coming with us is that he gets seasick. I wish we'd never gotten mixed up with him. I don't like the idea of kidnapping children. That's a federal crime, you know. And how are we supposed to find El Rosario? We don't have any proper charts, he only gave us a Rand McNally highway map and a sketch of the shoreline. That dope has no idea at all of sailing or navigation."

"Well, neither do you, Al," cut in his companion. "We've never been outside the bay ourselves. How did we ever get into this mess anyway?"

"We were drunk, and you were bragging about what a good sailor you were. Don't you remember? He offered to 'pay us well for a little job'—those were his exact words. Everything is a bit fuzzy after that, but the next morning we found ourselves stuck here, wherever or whenever here is. Maybe he took us into the past when the bay was still here, but there was no city. Come on. Let's get back to the boat."

Susan waited until the dinghy was bumping up against the ship before she scurried back up the hill to her brother and her friend. Quietly the three of them discussed what to do.

William wanted to head straight back to the exit vortex and into San Francisco to tell Mr. and Mrs. Wilson what they had learned. Harold was afraid that Hagen might booby-trap the exit to blow up anyone else who tried to use it. That possibility had not occurred to any of them before. Susan was worried about the children on the boat. "I don't trust those men to take proper care of the children." She said. "What if some of them get sick or die on the way to El Rosario? If we went on board, we could at least make sure they were not mistreated."

In the end they decided to talk to the sailors. They chose Harold as their spokesman, since he was the oldest. When they reached the shore, they began waving their arms to attract attention. They had decided not to shout, just in case Hagen still happened to be nearby. Within a few minutes the men on the boat were headed their way in the dinghy.

"Hey, you must be the kids the Boss was asking about," said Al. "Well, come on, we'll take you on out to the boat with the rest of them."

Harold answered, "We didn't come to be locked up in the hold of your boat with the rest of the children. We came to make sure they get home safely, and perhaps we can also help you."

The short man laughed loudly, "Hey, that's a pretty good pretty good one. Do you have any more funny stories? Let's just grab them, Pete." The two men stepped out of the dinghy and started toward the children, but after two steps they ran into a soft, yet solid wall. They pushed, they pounded, they shouted. They tried to go left, they tried to go right, they tried to retreat. Five minutes later --tired, sweating, frustrated and fearful--they leaned against their soft prison wall for a rest. At that moment the children spoke a few words in the Mother Tongue, and the air shield collapsed, sending the men tumbling to the ground.

The tall man, Pete, began to swear, but Harold cut him short. "Stop. Are you ready to talk, or do you want something more painful?" Pete and his buddy Al stood up slowly and then nodded for Harold to continue.

"As we see it," he said, "there are three possibilities. First, we can take you and the children back to San Francisco immediately. The problem is that we don't know where Hagen is. He might be waiting for us there, or he might have booby-trapped the exit. The second possibility is to wait here for my parents. We sent them a message, and they may come for us in the next few hours. We hope they will check out the exit from this place before they try to follow us here. The problem with this plan is that Hagen may come back and secretly watch for your departure before my parents arrive. The last alternative we can think of is to come with you to El Rosario. You can sail the boat; we will help out however we can, and we will try to make sure the children are okay. If we go with you, then my parents will have time to call in reinforcements to deal with Hagen at El Rosario. We can't make up our mind about what is best, so we wanted to see what you would suggest. I don't like standing here in the open, though, with Hagen on the loose. We should probably go out to the sailboat to talk."

"Wow! You kids are really something!" exclaimed Pete. "You're no older than the ones we have on board, and now you're taking over? Who are you? Or what are you? How did you put us in that invisible box? Was it magic?"

"No," said Harold. "It was not magic. It was knowledge. We are just normal, human children, who have received some extraordinary training. We are afraid of Hagen because he is stronger and knows much more than we do, but we have come because we love and serve God. Jesus said, 'The wind blows where it wishes and you hear the sound of it, but do not know where it comes from and where it is going; so is everyone who is born of the Spirit' (John 3:8). God's Spirit sometimes takes God's children places where they would never have gone by themselves. We are here because God has brought us here. Now, will you please take us out to your boat?"

Al and Pete nodded together. With new respect they waited until the boys had climbed into the dinghy, and then Pete lifted Susan aboard so that she wouldn't wet her feet. As the men rowed, the children told the amazed sailors about rescuing Andrea and how they had also been rescued from drowning. They explained how they had hidden from Hagen and how Susan had managed to over hear their conversation at the shore.

Once on board the children and the men discussed the alternatives Harold had suggested. The men were afraid to disobey Hagen's order to sail and so were the children, so it really did not take too long to come to a decision. The children would hide on board so that Hagen could not see them if he returned, but they would also watch carefully for Harold's parents. If the Wilsons had not come by the turning of the tide, the boat and its cargo of children would set sail.

For the next couple of hours the children anxiously scanned the shore, but neither Hagen, nor the Wilsons showed up. Finally, a little after 3:00 o'clock in the afternoon Pete and Al pulled up the anchor, raised the sail and turned toward the mouth of San Francisco bay.

CHAPTER 6—SEASICK

The boat was not like any the children had seen during their walk beside the bay on the day before. It was about thirty feet long and wider than most modern boats that size. It had a flat deck surrounded by a wooden railing, to which six large wooden water casks were tied. Two square covers, called hatches, one fore and one aft, provided the only access to the area below the deck.

A single mast rose just ahead of the middle of the deck. The mast was shorter than the children expected, and at its top a long wooden cross beam was suspended. The beam, which slanted down towards the bow and up away from the stern, supported a large, orange, triangular sail.

Harold, Susan, and William watched as Pete worked to pull the sail around to catch the breeze while Al held the tiller that moved the boat's rudder. Both men were muttering under their breath. Harold leaned over and whispered to Susan, "Our friends don't know what they're doing." Susan nodded.

It took over three hours of floundering about to get past the Golden Gate and out into the open sea. On two occasions, the children held their breath as the vessel nearly crashed into rocky cliffs. When they were well out of the harbor, and had turned south, Harold walked over to Al and asked, "We're pretty tired and hungry. Where is the food; where are the beds, and where are the rest of the children?"

"Pete and I can't do anything for you now. We have never been on a sailboat like this. It doesn't work at all like the little day sailers that we have used inside the bay, so he can't leave the ropes, and I can't leave the tiller. The kids are under there." He pointed to the aft hatch. "The grub is up front where Pete and I have our bunks. I don't know when we'll get to use them now. You can toss two or three of loaves of bread down to the kids. Pull up their slop bucket and dump it over the side. Fill up their water bucket at the cask over there."

Harold, Susan, and William went to check on the children, but when they removed the hatch, the smell was so terrible that William immediately became sick and had to put his head over the side-rail. Twenty-four children were all crammed into a room six feet high, twelve feet long and ten feet wide at its maximum width. Some of them had been sick and not all of them had made it over to the slop bucket.

Susan stepped back from the opening, gasped for breath, and then leaned over the hole. "We have come to help you. I don't think we can do much today, but tomorrow we will. I promise."

There was no ladder down into the room, so Harold pulled up the slop bucket with a rope, washed it with seawater and lowered it down again. Then he pulled up the water bucket and filled it. Meanwhile, Susan had gone to look for food. The forward compartment was a terrible mess. Hundreds of cans of soup, stew, spaghetti, and various kinds of fruit were all jumbled together. Six loaves of stale bread rested on top of the heap. Susan dropped four of them down the hole, and Harold fastened the hatch back over the children. She gave bread and water to the two sailors; then she and Harold helped William to crawl down through the forward hatch.

On his way down Harold grabbed the bolt for the hatch so the men would not be able to lock them in. Susan and Harold had bread and water for supper, but William was still sick, so he refused to eat anything. Then the three of them collapsed together into a pile of blankets all the way up in the pointed bow of the boat.

When they woke up, a shaft of sunlight was pouring in

through the open hatch and Al was asleep on one of the side berths. When they sat up, he stirred, opened his eyes and groaned, "Ooohhh! Guess I'd better go topside and see how Pete is doing." As Al explained later, the wind had been steady all night and the seas fairly calm, so the men had been able to take turns sleeping.

Then Harold and Susan found a can opener and ate a can of peaches along with some stale bread. William was fine as long as he lay down, but his stomach started doing flip-flops as soon as he sat up, so he passed on breakfast. After eating, Susan pulled Frigga's devotional book out of her purse.

"Our passage for this morning comes from Mark 10:43-45," she said. "Whoever wishes to become great among you shall be your servant; and whoever wishes to be first among you shall be slave of all. For even the Son of Man did not come to be served, but to serve, and to give His life a ransom for many."

"I never thought of Jesus as a servant before," remarked Harold. "After all, He is the Lord."

"Yes, I know, it is strange," replied Susan, "Maybe our book's comments will help us understand. Listen. 'Jesus served us by dying for us,'" she read, "'but He also served people every day. He did not order them to bring Him money and wait on Him hand and foot. Instead, He healed them and helped them for free even when He was tired. Jesus told His disciples to act the same way. After His death and resurrection the apostles were strong leaders of the early church, but they were also servants. They served Christ, and they served the church.'"

When Susan had finished reading, Harold sat very still for a few minutes thinking about what he had heard. Finally, he stirred, smiled at Susan, and said, "Thanks. Let's pray."

After they had prayed, Harold got a rope ladder from Pete, pulled up the hatch over the children's quarters, and using the ladder climbed down into smelly hole. He helped as Susan hauled both buckets up to the deck. Then he turned to examine the children. Several of them looked sick and pale; the littlest one, a boy of about four began to cry for his mommy. The rest either sat or stood and stared at Harold.

"My name is Harold," he began. "My friends Susan, William and I came from San Francisco to find you and to take you home. Before we can do that, we will have to go on a long sea voyage. We are counting on our parents and some of our friends to capture the man who kidnapped you and to meet us at the end of the voyage. The two men up there—Pete and Al— are in charge of sailing the boat, but Susan, William and I have come to serve you. We will work hard and do everything we can to make things easier for you, but you must do what we say. So I am your boss and your servant at the same time. Do you understand?"

"That's dumb," sneered a tall boy in ragged jeans. "You can't be the boss and a servant. I can beat you up with one hand tied behind my back. So let's just turn things around a bit. I'll be the boss, and you be the servant." The boy stepped up to face Harold. He was at least two inches taller than Harold.

Harold sighed. "Okay. I didn't want to do this, but let's have it out right here and now. Go ahead. Hit me in the face as hard as you can." The boy doubled up his fist and punched hard, right at Harold's nose, but Harold's nose wasn't there. At the last instant Harold moved to one side. As the boy stumbled off balance, Harold grabbed his outstretched arm, pulled it down and flipped the boy onto his back.

The boy struggled to his feet, more angry than hurt, and picked up a large board that had been leaning against the wall. As he swung it toward Harold's head, Harold did not move at all. He merely whispered a few words in the Mother Tongue to make a hard air shield (as opposed to the soft kind). The board struck the shield a quarter inch above his head and broke. To everyone in the little cabin, it looked as if Harold's head had been hit, but he just smiled and said, "Is that the best you can do?"

The other boy stood and stared with his mouth open for a few seconds. Then he dropped the piece of board still in his hand and shrugged. "Okay. So you're the boss."

Harold held out his hand for a high-five. The other boy gave it a resounding slap and grinned, "My name's Mike. What do you want me to do?"

"What I want," said Harold, "is for you to help me serve these kids. We need to care for the little ones and the weak ones. I want every one of them to get home safely. To start with, Susan will send down a better breakfast than you have been getting. Then we need to wash this room and maybe some of the clothes that you guys are wearing. This place smells awful. I want everyone to go up on deck for part of the day. If you are all topside at the same time, you will be in the way, but I think it will be all right if you take turns, eight of you at a time. Later, maybe tomorrow, we need to organize the canned food."

Over the next few hours Harold and Susan worked very hard. So did Mike who had become completely devoted to Harold. All the children called Harold, "Boss," as he organized the work and assigned tasks. Quite a few of them insisted on calling Susan an angel. She had a gentle touch and a kind word for every child, especially the little ones. By lunchtime she had learned all of their names and knew something about each one. Even the older boys and girls followed her around and competed for the privilege of helping her because when she smiled at them, the icy fear in their hearts began to melt away.

By mid-afternoon the children's room and the filthiest of their clothes had been thoroughly scrubbed with salt-water. The children were all very tired, so Harold sent them down for a rest before supper. He and Susan were exhausted, but happy.

As they sat leaning against the mast, Al came up and squatted down in front of them. "I want to thank you for all you have done," he said. "I know that Pete and I weren't doing right by those kids. We didn't intend to be cruel, but, well. . . thanks. And there's one more thing. You said that God had sent you here. I believe He did, but I still don't understand why you are putting your lives in danger and why you are working so hard. I've never seen any children like you before, or even any older people."

"Jesus Christ served and helped people even when He was tired," said Harold. "Then He died on the cross to pay the penalty for our sins. Three days later He rose up again from the grave. Susan and William and I have received Jesus as our Savior, so He has forgiven us all for our sins. He also sent His Holy Spirit into our hearts to make us more like Himself. So when we serve and help these children, it is really Jesus in us who is at work. He is doing in us the same kinds of things He did when He walked on the Earth. We still have problems just as other children do. Sometimes we get mad at each other, and we do lots of wrong things, but Jesus has made a difference in our lives."

Susan leaned forward and gently touched Al's face with her hand. She looked straight into his eyes and said softly, "Al, I hope that you will repent of your sins and trust Jesus to save you as we have done. Will you promise me that you will think about it?"

A large tear trickled down each cheek as Al answered, "Yes, Miss. Yes, I will." Then he stood and walked across the deck to trim the sail.

Susan and Harold leaned back against the mast and dozed for a few minutes, but they woke up when the wind shifted and the sailors brought the boat around on another tack. "Let's go check on William again," said Harold. "I have an idea that may help him."

William was not much better, and he listened attentively as Harold explained his idea. "Do you remember how old Ulysses is?"

"Yes. Last summer he told our parents that he was four hundred and seventy three. I guess he may be a year older by now, but so what?"

"Well, the people of Earth-Two use their knowledge of the Mother Tongue to help them fight disease and to keep themselves from aging as quickly as people in our world. So they must be able to tell their bodies what to do. If you use the Mother Tongue and command your stomach to be still, maybe it will listen to you."

William lay back amidst the blankets and began to concentrate. He knew that using the Mother Tongue was not just a matter of saying the right words. The words were not magical spells that produced results even if the speaker did not understand them. So William closed his eyes and concentrated; he tried to locate the exact place in his body where the nausea began; he tried to trace its path throughout his body. He focused in turn on his stomach, his throat and mouth, his head. Finally he spoke in a firm and confident voice the ancient words, which we translate as, "Be still." A few moments later he sat up and exclaimed, "I'm hungry!"

William ate and felt fine, so he helped distribute supper to the children in their quarters. Some of them were still too seasick to eat more than a few bites, but he patiently helped and encouraged them to take as much as they could tolerate. Later that night as he lay down to sleep an idea began to form in his mind. The next morning he decided to try it out. He asked Harold and Mike to bring the sickest child up on deck. It was a little girl about six years old. Kneeling down beside her he placed his hands on her head, closed his eyes and concentrated on her stomach, her throat and mouth, her head. Then, speaking firmly in the Mother Tongue, he said, "Be still."

He opened his eyes, looked at the girl, and said, "Try to sit up. How do you feel?"

Her eyes were wide with amazement as she replied, "I'm hungry!"

Over the course of the next hour William treated five other children who were suffering from nausea. Susan and Harold tried to help him, but they were unsuccessful, so William had to care for the children by himself. By the time he was finished, he was so tired and hungry he could hardly stand up. Over the course of their journey William was able to help several of the children (and even Pete) with minor pains or upset stomachs, and that is how he became the doctor for the voyage.

Much later, after their adventure was over, Frigga talked to them about William's ability. "It is a very rare gift," she said. "Many people on Earth-Two learn to focus their minds on the healing of their own bodies. That is how they fight infection or headaches or nausea. Only a very few are able to do things to the bodies of other people by using the Mother Tongue. Hagen has that gift. That is the reason he was able to knock you unconscious with only a few words. In his case the gift is wasted because he has used it for evil. But William has a great opportunity to develop his gift for good."

"Is that how people in the Bible performed miracles?" asked Susan. "Were they using their minds along with the Mother Tongue?"

"Oh no," replied Frigga. "The Mother Tongue does not give anyone that kind of ability. No one can use the Mother Tongue to part the sea or to make the sun stand still or to heal someone born blind or lame or to raise the dead. Those things were miracles of God. The doctors on your Earth know that when people are cheerful and expect to get well they are more likely to recover than if they are depressed and anxious. Our minds affect our bodies and the Mother Tongue simply increases that ability. God's miracles, however, are wonderful demonstrations of His power, and we must always trust in Him, not in ourselves."

CHAPTER 7—THE STORM

After the first couple of days, life fell into a regular routine. Before breakfast Susan read to the children and the sailors from her devotional book. Then Harold or William prayed. After that Harold assigned chores. These did not take very long, but they made all of the children feel as if they were an important part of the expedition. Games, talking or just looking at the beauty of sea and sky filled in the rest of the day.

Some of the older children learned to help work the lines attached to the sail and to steer the boat with the tiller, so they were able to relieve Pete and Al, at least when the weather was fair. The general plan was to head south, keeping the coast of California within sight, but Pete and Al had one major concern. How would they know when they were close enough to El Rosario to begin searching the shoreline for the landmarks that Hagen had sketched? Al explained the problem to Harold, Susan, and William on the second morning after their departure from San Francisco.

"All we have is this Rand McNally Road Atlas. Since the city of San Francisco has disappeared, I don't suppose Santa Barbara or Los Angeles or San Diego is still around either. We might recognize some of the larger islands off the coast of southern California if it isn't night when we pass them, or maybe we will be able to find San Diego bay. Even if we do, there aren't many landmarks south of that, and El Rosario isn't right on the coast, if the town is even there. Do you have any ideas?"

"May I see the atlas?" asked William. He looked at it very carefully while the others talked. "What are these tiny numbers over in the margin?" he asked after a few minutes. "They are so faint I didn't notice them at first."

"Oh, those show the latitude," replied Al. "Do you see the raised zero after each number? That means degrees. See, San Francisco is a little less than thirty-eight degrees north latitude. If we had some way of figuring out our latitude, we would know where we were."

"My science teacher showed us how to do that," said Harold. "We can use a protractor to figure out many degrees high in the sky the North Star is. That is our latitude."[2]

"We don't have a protractor," growled Al. "We don't even have a compass. I told Hagen we needed more stuff, and he promised to bring it. I even asked for a book on navigation, but then you three showed up, and that changed everything."

"I think I can make a protractor," said Susan. Susan was in honors math, and she had already taken some geometry. "I can draw it on the cardboard from one of the cereal boxes in our pantry. Let's see, a right angle is ninety degrees; half of that is forty-five; half of forty-five is twenty-two and a half. Then I can draw an equilateral triangle; each angle will be 60 degrees and half of that is thirty. . . ." She wandered off muttering to herself while the others continued discussing their voyage. By supper time she had made two very large protractors out of cardboard.

"Why two," asked William?

"To check myself," she answered. I wanted to make sure that I didn't make any mistakes, so I used a slightly different procedure on the second one. I'm quite pleased. They line up perfectly. Anyway, now we have a spare in case one gets wet."

That night the sky was clear, and the sea was calm, so they took three measurements. Amazingly enough, they agreed fairly well. "If this is right," said Pete, "we should see Morro Bay

---

[2] If you want to know how to use a protractor to find your latitude, look in Appendix 2 at the end of the story.

sometime tomorrow." And they did. Pete recognized the place because a friend had once taken him ocean fishing there. From a distance William thought Morro Rock looked like the top of the head of a giant, who was trying to break free from an underground prison. Since the area appeared to be deserted, they anchored not far shore. That night Harold and the two men rowed to the Rock to check the position of the North Star from dry ground instead of from the moving deck of the sailboat. Their results agreed quite well with the map, so they all felt much more confident as they headed south early the next morning.

The weather continued fair all that day, but the next morning was gray, gloomy and windy. The Scripture portion from Susan's devotional booklet was Psalm 107:23-30.

Those who go down to the sea in ships,
Who do business on great waters;
They have seen the works of the LORD,
And His wonders in the deep.
For He spoke and raised up a stormy wind,
Which lifted up the waves of the sea.
They rose up to the heavens, they went down to the depths;
Their soul melted away in their misery.
They reeled and staggered like a drunken man,
And were at their wits' end.
Then they cried to the LORD in their trouble,
And He brought them out of their distresses.
He caused the storm to be still,
So that the waves of the sea were hushed.
Then they were glad because they were quiet,
So He guided them to their desired haven.

The booklet went on to compare a storm at sea with the stormy problems people have in their daily lives on land. When she finished reading, it was William's turn to pray, and he said, "Dear heavenly Father, please do not send a terrible storm while we are in this boat, but if You do, we ask you to take care of us and to bring us all safely through it. Thank you for the good weather we have enjoyed so far. In Jesus' name, Amen."

As the day wore on, the sky became even darker, and the waves began to slam their fists into the side of the boat. All of the children except Harold, Susan, and William were confined below the deck, and even they stayed below for much of the day. Al and Pete kept close to shore as they looked for a safe harbor. Twice they thought they saw a possibility, but strong gusts of wind from the shore kept them from bringing the boat around. By four o'clock the wind was so strong that the sail had to be rolled up to prevent it from being torn to shreds. Without a sail to stabilize it, the boat began wallowing sideways in the waves, rocking violently as it slid from peak to trough to peak to trough. Both hatches had to be closed to prevent the cabins from being flooded by the waves that broke over the side. Susan and William went to the aft compartment, trying to comfort the frightened children, while Harold did what he could to help Pete and Al.

About five o'clock Harold ducked down into the forward compartment to get food for anyone who felt like eating. (Most did not.) When he lifted the hatch again, he saw Pete and Al at the stern of the boat, pulling on the rope that held the shore boat. "Hey, what are you guys doing?" he shouted. Pete looked back but did not answer. Harold hopped out, fastened the hatch and went back as quickly as he could along the rolling deck. "What are you doing?" he asked again.

Al refused to look at Harold, but Pete snarled, "We're getting out of here. Every minute the land gets farther away. We can't do anything with this tub of a sailboat, but we can row ourselves to shore—if we hurry."

"If you leave, everyone on board will drown. We can't manage the boat by ourselves. You must stay."

"Says who?" grunted Pete, as he turned back to his task.

Harold crawled over to the aft hatch, lifted it up and called down, "Susan, William. I need you. Right away."

When they were topside, he quickly explained the situation. "So what should we do?" he asked. "If we put them in an air shield, we will have to use all of our strength just to maintain the shield. We won't be able to do much else."

"Let me try Hagen's trick," suggested William. "I remember what he said to knock us out, and I think I can see what he did with his mind." At Harold's nod, William stepped up behind the two men and uttered a short phrase in the Mother Tongue with a loud, commanding voice. On the last syllable both men fell to the deck unconscious.

"I don't think it will last very long," said William. "Perhaps we should tie them up. Hagen didn't think of much, but at least he made sure there was duct tape aboard."

Within five minutes Pete and Al were trussed up like two turkeys ready for roasting, except—as Harold noted—melted duct tape would not taste very good on a turkey. A few minutes later both men woke up. When they started grumbling and swearing, Harold threatened to toss them over the side, so they shut up. Meanwhile the storm was getting worse, and the deck was heaving so much from side to side that the children could not stand up without holding on to something.

"Let's pray," suggested Susan as they sat huddled together on the deck. "Dear Father," she said, "we come to you just like those sailors in the Psalm. Please rescue us as you rescued them. Please show us if there is anything we can do to keep from sinking. In Jesus name, Amen."

After a few moments, Harold said, "I have an idea. Last fall I read a bunch of stories about Admiral Horatio Hornblower. One time he was out in a storm like this, and he cut down one of the masts and let it drag behind his ship. That made the ship turn so that the wind and waves came from behind. He saved the ship from being swamped by waves coming over the side. Maybe we could do something like that with the dinghy. Right now it has only one line tied to its bow. If we tie another to its stern and fill it with water, it may have enough drag enough to turn us around."

It took them nearly half an hour to put Harold's plan into effect. The deck was heaving from side to side, and the dinghy was too heavy for them to pull on board. Finally Harold had to climb over the edge, drop into the dinghy and tie on the stern line. There was already quite a bit of water in the little boat, but he used a bucket to fill it up. By that time he was sopping wet and nearly frozen, and it was all he could do to climb back up over the railing. Susan and William let the sinking dinghy drift about fifty feet away. Then, following Harold's directions, they tied off the lines on the starboard side of the boat near the stern. "Admiral Hornblower didn't want the waves coming straight behind his ship," he explained. "They should hit us slightly to one side of the stern."

Almost immediately the boat began to turn. William started jumping up and down, shouting in great excitement, "We did it! We did it!" But then, as though it resented being defeated, the angry sea cast its largest wave over the side of the boat. Suddenly the deck was awash with over a foot of water. The boat shuddered from stem to stern with the fearful pounding, and when the water had drained away, William was gone.

CHAPTER 8—A STRANGE BOAT

Susan and Harold raced to the railing. "William," wailed Susan. He was nowhere to be seen. Susan grabbed Harold's hand. "The Mother Tongue. Let's call him with the Mother Tongue."

"I can't, Susan. It's all I can do just to stand here. I'm so tired."

Susan looked up at him. He had been brave for so long, but he was only eleven and she was only ten. They were just children after all, and they were at the end of their strength. She put her arm around his waist and pulled his arm across her shoulder. "Please, Harold, try."

He nodded and together they faced the hungry sea that had devoured her brother and his friend. Just at that moment, the churning waters spit William to the top of a wave about halfway to the submerged dinghy. With one voice and one heart Harold and Susan cried out in the Mother Tongue, "William, rise!" Slowly their wills pulled him up from the clinging waves. Then in the same Tongue they called, "William, come!" And he came—floating over the water, and over the railing, and into the arms of Susan and Harold.

The three children collapsed together into a soggy, motionless heap. Darkness settled over them, and they did not move. The wind grew less; the waves grew calm, and the children lay as still as three sleeping logs.

Susan's dreams were filled with rushing water and black fear and cries that echoed off into silence: "William, William, William! Harold, Harold, Harold!" But then there was an echo that grew louder, "Susan, Susan, Susan!"

Susan's eyes popped open. It was Al. He was still trussed up like a turkey, wrapped in duct tape, but he had managed to wriggle his way across the deck, and he was looking down at her in deep concern. Behind his head the sky was a dull gray. She tried to move, but William was lying across her right leg, which had gone numb, so she rolled him off with a shove and struggled to a sitting position. Her movements roused the boys. Soon all three of them were sitting up yawning and rubbing various sore spots.

"We were afraid you were all dead," said Al. "I'm very sorry. We both are, for trying to leave the boat. Our bodies may be bigger than yours, but our hearts are certainly smaller. Pete and I are ready to swear obedience to you, Harold. For as long as this voyage lasts, you are our captain."

Harold did not reply, but he crawled over and cut both Al and Pete free with his pocketknife. Although the men were stiff and sore, they could see that Harold, Susan, and William were still too exhausted to do anything, so they fed the children in the aft cabin and brought them all up on deck for a special ceremony. With Harold seated on a water cask and Susan and William standing beside him, Pete and Al knelt on the deck and pledged their allegiance to the three children, and especially to Harold as the new captain. Pete had found a grocery sack full of lunch puddings in the pantry, so these were distributed as a special treat.

The pudding lifted everyone's mood a bit, but they were all cold and wet, and a great many buckets full of water had to be hauled out of both cabins. Pete and Al dragged the dinghy back to its proper place, and Mike volunteered to bail it out while the two men unfurled the sail. As the brisk breeze filled the sail, the boat became more stable in the water, and those with queasy stomachs felt much better.

Throughout the morning's labors, Harold, William and Susan had been sitting up near the bow of the boat. They talked little, and stared much at the sullen sea and sky.

"Which way, Captain?" Al's voice jerked Harold out of his moody reverie. "Which way do you want us to head? The storm pushed us out of sight of land, and we can't see the sun because of the clouds. We think the wind shifted several times during the night, so it may not be coming from the east any more. I sure wish we had a compass."

Harold nodded. "Thanks, Al, for everything you and Pete have done this morning. I don't know what is wrong with me. I feel as gray as the sky and as weak as a wet noodle." Susan and William grunted their agreement. "Doesn't your weather pretty often come from the west or northwest?" he continued. "If we keep the wind behind us, we have a good chance of heading east or southeast toward the coast."

"Thanks, Captain. That's what we thought, too. Bye the way, I'm sure you will all feel better tomorrow after a good night's rest."

Although Al and Pete did their best to keep the rest of the children occupied, the gloomy faces of Harold, Susan, and William affected everyone on board, and soon the other children began to bicker among themselves. At last Pete tired of the constant parade of complaining little tattletales, and he sent all of the children down into their room. "Go ahead and fight all you want," he said as he closed the hatch over their heads. "At least I won't be able to hear you."

It was past time for supper when Al lowered himself through the forward hatch to look for Susan. She was lying in her berth, not sleeping, but simply staring at the wall. She and Harold had quarreled, and when William took Harold's side, she had gone below to cry. "Begging your pardon, Miss, but I think maybe we didn't start the day out right. I think we're all missing the reading and the prayer. Most of the children are crying, and Pete is as grumpy as an old mule. Would you please come and read from your little book?"

Susan lay still with her face turned toward the wall. "Please, Miss. I need it too. I'll go up and talk to the boys about praying."

Two or three minutes later Susan emerged from the cabin, clutching her precious booklet from Frigga. Harold and William were waiting for her. "Without Mom and Dad, you guys are all that I have," she whispered.

"I know," said Harold. "I'm sorry. We've got to stick together." He put one arm around her and another around William, and the three children clung to each other. Susan and William cried softly, and even Harold's eyes glistened with tears. After a few minutes they walked back to lift the aft hatch. When all of the children were up on deck, Harold said, "I know this has been a rough day for all of us, and I suppose we are all a little bit afraid because we can't see land. I'm sure you miss your parents just as we do. Susan, William and I have been crabby all day, and that has made things worse. Still, we can thank God for bringing us all safely through the storm, and we can commit the rest of this day back to God who gave it. Susan, will you please read to us?"

"Our Bible verse for the day is 1 Timothy 1:15, 'It is a trustworthy statement, deserving full acceptance, that Christ Jesus came into the world to save sinners, among whom I am foremost of all.'" Susan looked up briefly at Al; then she continued reading. "'Jesus did not come into the world to save good people. He came to save sinners. He came to save murderers, thieves, liars and people who take God's name in vain. Some people do not believe they are sinners, but the Bible says that 'all have sinned and fall short of the glory of God.' God does not love people because they are good. He loves them in order to make them good. When a sinner trusts in the death and resurrection of Jesus Christ, God forgives all of his sins.

Then he begins a new life in God's family with a new home awaiting him in heaven.'"

Susan closed the book, looked straight at Al and said, "If anyone here wants to receive Jesus as his Savior, we will be glad to help him." She continued looking at Al, her eyes pleading with him, until William stood up to pray. As he prayed, a new stillness settled down over the little company of men and children, and when they opened their eyes, the petty quarrels of the day seemed faint and far away.

Later that evening after most of the children had gone to bed, Al walked over to where Harold and Susan were leaning against the railing. "Miss," he began.

"Yes, Al."

"I want to become a Christian."

And so it was that Harold and Susan led him to pray, "Dear Father in heaven, I know I have sinned and that I deserve to be punished in hell for my sins. Thank you for sending Jesus to die and to pay the penalty for my sins. Thank you for raising Him from the grave so that He can give me new life. I now turn from my sins and receive Jesus as my Savior. In His name I pray, Amen."

When they raised their heads, six eyes were moist with tears, but none of them saw the others because of the darkness. The next morning before the reading and prayer, Al confessed his new faith in Christ before everyone aboard, which encouraged several of the children to trust in the Lord Jesus as well. Harold, Susan, and William discovered that the cloud had lifted completely from their hearts, and in spite of the gray skies and chilly breeze they were very happy.

About ten o'clock William was leaning on the forward railing scanning the horizon with the binoculars. "Come, look, Harold. Over there." Harold took the binoculars and swept across the area William had indicated. "Do you see them?" asked William.

"I think so. I see little specks in the sky. Are they birds? Seagulls, maybe?"

"Yes. And where there are birds, there should be land."

Harold called back to Pete, who was at the helm. "Turn the boat to port. We see birds."

"Aye, aye, Captain." Pete grinned and pushed the tiller to starboard, then straightened it out again when William indicated that they were on course.

News of the birds brought all of the children up on deck, and of course everyone had to have a look. At noon Al took the binoculars from the last (and smallest) of the young observers. Almost immediately he announced that he could see land. By two o'clock all of the taller children could see land without the binoculars. Shortly after that the sun broke through the clouds and it became clear that they were heading west by northwest into a small group of islands.

At three o'clock Pete tapped Harold on the shoulder and led him away from the crowded railing. "Captain," he whispered, "I just spotted a large ship through the glasses. It is square rigged with two masts. It looks to be a lot faster and a lot bigger than we are, and it is headed straight toward us."

Harold stepped up into the rigging for a better view. As he focused on the approaching ship, his stomach began turning and churning. "Susan. William. Please come here. There's another ship headed our way. I have a bad feeling about it, and I think we should send the children below. Don't tell them why just yet, or they will all want to stay up and see it."

There was a fair amount of grumbling about the Captain's orders, but all of the children were safely below before any of them had noticed the strange ship. By four o'clock it was less than a mile away and the binoculars showed its decks crowded with armed men. Most held a naked sword. Several men with bows stood beside fire pots ready to ignite flaming arrows. "Can we outrun them?" Harold asked.

"I don't think so, Captain," answered Pete.

"Ok. Turn us into the wind. We'll stop here and wait for them."

CHAPTER 9—INTO THE LIONS' DEN

As the strange ship approached, Harold said to Pete and Al, "Susan, William and I will probably be able to understand most of what they are saying, but I don't want to let on that we know anything until we figure out what their intentions are. I want you, Pete, to act as if you are in charge. The three of us will listen and try to keep you two informed. For now, let's just put our hands up in the air so they can see we are carrying no weapons."

At this sign of surrender the men on the ship lowered their swords and bows. When only a few feet separated the two vessels, sailors jumped across the gap and tied them together. The men were dressed in loose-fitting pantaloons tied about the waist with a cord. Brightly colored shirts of red, blue, yellow or green were tucked in at the waist, and most of them wore gold chains around their necks and wrists. Their captain stood a good three inches taller than any of the other men; he was broad across the shoulders and very loud of mouth. As he shouted orders at his crew, the children listened carefully, but most of it was sailor talk, and they did not know all of the words.

Pete stepped forward, spread out his hands, palms up, in a gesture of peace and asked, "What do you want, sir?" The captain simply scowled at this thin man in the strange clothes who spoke in a strange tongue. When Pete repeated his question, the pirate slammed the back of his fist across Pete's mouth and sent him stumbling across the deck. Then he ordered his men to search for cargo.

"Children! Children! Is that all?" he shouted? "Bring them up on deck. Bring everything up!" As the foodstuffs were tossed up, he grabbed a can of stew in each hand, shoved them at Pete and demanded, "What are these useless things? Where is your gold? Where is your silver? Where is the rest of your fleet? Lost in the storm?" When Pete just shrugged, he threw the cans down in anger, stomped to the stern and sat down on a water keg.

The pirates clustered around their captain and began to argue amongst themselves, so with a look and a nod Harold sent Susan and William back to listen. They drifted idly toward the stern, mixing in with the other children. After a few minutes William returned to report. "They know we are not from their Earth, but they cannot decide what we are doing here. Because we have so many children on board, some are arguing that our Earth is overcrowded and that we are part of a colonizing expedition. The rest think we are hostages or slaves captured in a raid on our Earth by a colony up north. Either prospect seems to frighten them because they think it must take great knowledge and power to pass between the worlds."

"What do you mean, 'pass between the worlds?'" asked Al. "I always assumed we were on the same planet, but in a different time."

"We will explain later if our parents think it is wise," replied Harold. "Go ahead, William."

"The captain and most of the crew are in favor of tossing us overboard and taking our boat, but the old man, the one with the white hair, is arguing against them. He says we should be taken to their council of elders. I didn't catch everything, but I think he was threatening to bring charges before the council if the captain did not listen."

"That is right, William," said Susan, coming up behind him. "The captain is not happy about it, but he has given in. Part of his crew will be left on board to sail us into their harbor."

Within a few minutes, both vessels were headed toward the cluster of islands. Susan herded most of the children back into their quarters, but she kept several of the older ones up to help replace the food in the forward cabin. Then she served supper. The Earth-Two sailors aboard were greatly interested in the process of opening canned food, but when Susan offered them some, only one was willing to try it.

It was nearly dark by the time they were anchored in the harbor of the westernmost of the three larger islands. "If we were back home, Captain, I would say that these are the Channel Islands off Santa Barbara and that this is Santa Cruz Island," said Al as he handed the atlas to Harold.

Harold started to reply, but at that moment a thud announced the arrival of the pirate captain in his ship's rowboat. He climbed aboard, shoved Pete and Al toward the railing and indicated that they should climb down the rope ladder.

"I don't like for us to be split up," whispered Harold, "but I think I should go too. I don't want to leave our cargo of children alone, so William and Susan, will you please stay here? Pray for me." They nodded, and as Harold followed the pirate captain over the railing, Susan began to pray.

"Dear Lord, please protect Harold and our two friends. We have no idea of what they might be facing, but you do. Please give Harold wisdom through your Holy Spirit. In Jesus' name, amen."

The captain grunted in surprise when Harold dropped into the rowboat behind him, but he did not send him back. Although the shore was at least a half-mile away, the trip only took a few minutes because the boat was rowed by four strong seamen. As he splashed through the shallow water and up onto the beach, Harold examined the small cluster of buildings perched all higgledy-piggledy on the rocky shore. They were made of native stone with sloping roofs of rough-hewn boards. Flickering light shone from a few open windows, but most of the windows had been already been covered with heavy wooden shutters.

The three captives were prodded toward the largest of the buildings and through its open door into a long narrow room. The pirate captain led his small triumphal procession through the crowd that had already gathered. At the far end of the room seven aged men sat on seven intricately carved chairs, which were placed on a raised platform. To this platform the captives were led, and before it they were forced to kneel. At a nod from the old man in the center of the platform, the captain began to speak.

"I thank you, my lords, for calling a council so quickly. As you know, I sailed this afternoon to capture a prize, but when we reached it we found no booty, only these two men and a number of children aboard. As you can see, they are strangely dressed. They do not appear to understand our language, and they speak among themselves in a different tongue. This can only mean one thing. They come from Earth-One, and we may be in danger from whoever has learned to pass between the worlds."

At this announcement, a murmur of surprise rippled through the crowd. The president of the council held up his hand for quiet. "Have you any more to report, captain?"

"Only this. I believe it would be folly to let them go and reveal our location to their friends. Most of my men think we should put all of the captives to death. If necessary, we can burn their boat to destroy all evidence of their passing this way. A few of them, however, have counseled that we keep them as hostages in case we are attacked."

"You have done well to bring them before us, Captain. I would have expected you to toss them all overboard. Perhaps you are growing in wisdom after all. Now, if any of you citizens wish to speak, you have the permission of the council."

For the next hour Harold listened as first one and then another of the villagers spoke. Some favored execution; others suggested that the children be adopted, and a few even urged the colony to end piracy altogether. The overriding emotion of the assembly, however, was fear, fear of Earth-One and fear of powerful individuals, who could travel between the worlds.

Finally Harold stood. The palms of his hands were sweaty, and his stomach was knotted with anxiety as he began, "Most excellent Lords and Councilors, I request permission to speak."

A gasp of surprise escaped from almost every throat at the same time. Only the president of the council smiled and nodded. "So you do understand us after all, young man. I wondered why you were here until I noticed that you alone of the captives were really listening to our debate. Yes, you may speak. What is your name, and what do you have to say for yourself?"

"My name is Harold. I speak the Mother Tongue and so do my friends Susan and William. These men and the rest of the children know nothing of your world or your language."

Harold briefly explained how they had first entered Earth-Two and then summarized their adventures in San Francisco and on the sea. "Now, my lords" he continued, "I want to talk about the fears of your people. They are right to be concerned about the safety of your village, but they do not understand yet exactly what they should fear. First of all, you should fear Hagen. I do not know how he obtained our boat, but I am sure it was in some evil way. If he is not captured, he could do much harm to your world and to ours. Second you should fear the ranger Ulysses. You may know him by another name, perhaps Odysseus or the Wanderer."

At this statement several of the councilors exchanged worried glances. "Yes," replied the president, "we have heard of the Wanderer."

"He is our friend and protector, and you should fear him more than you would fear any army. If we do not appear at the appointed rendezvous, he will scour the coast looking for word of us. You must have enemies, villages you have plundered, who will tell him where you are, and when he comes, he will know how to get the information he seeks. By himself, the Wanderer would be enough, but with him will be Frigga, who is our teacher and also a ranger. Finally, think of my parents and the parents of Susan and William. If there is need, they can bring terrible weapons of destruction from our world. These are the people you should fear, but with your permission I will also tell you how to escape your fears."

The president nodded, and Harold continued. "First you can send a boat with men to conduct us safely to our destination. Then you can help us capture Hagen and turn him over to the Wanderer. If you will do these things, and if you will turn away from piracy, I will ask the Wanderer to treat you with mercy. If you will not do these things, you have Someone even greater to fear. Jesus Christ said, 'Do not fear those who kill the body but are unable to kill the soul; but rather fear Him who is able to destroy both soul and body in hell' (Matthew 10:28). Jesus is the one who gives me courage to speak, and Jesus is the one who will judge your crimes if you do not repent and believe in Him."

The president and his council looked long at the boy standing before them. Finally the old man spoke. "You do not speak as a foolish child speaks, but with the boldness of a young man and with the wisdom of the aged. We will consider your words." Then in a louder voice he commanded, "Let the council chamber be cleared; let the prisoners be housed and well-treated until morning. We will summon you all again when we have reached our decision."

CHAPTER 10—THE TRAP IS SPRUNG

Susan slept uneasily that night. Dim and dreadful images dominated her dreams, until at last she woke to whisper into the darkness, "Harold! Harold! Are you back yet?" The only answer came from William.

"Are we going to make it home, Susan? Will we ever see Mom and Dad again? What has happened to Harold?" His voice was small and quavering. Susan could tell he was about to cry.

"I don't know, William. Do you want to come over here, little brother?" William crawled over to Susan's berth. He was trembling, but when she put her arms around him, he grew calm and fell asleep. She did not. The waning moon rose, poured its pale light through the open hatch and then moved toward the western horizon to make way for the sun. Susan noted its passing as she lay staring into the night. Her heart was troubled, but after a while she began to recite all of the verses she had memorized. When she came to Isaiah 26:3, she let it roll over and over in her thoughts.

The steadfast of mind You will keep in perfect peace,
Because he trusts in You.
The steadfast of mind You will keep in perfect peace,
Because he trusts in You.
The steadfast of mind You will keep in perfect peace,
Because he trusts in You.

Like a warm blanket on a cold night God's peace settled over her. As the first spear of light stabbed into the eastern sky, Susan's eyes finally closed in an exhausted and dreamless sleep.

Two hours later they were yanked open again by sounds from the deck above them. One of the pirate guards was shouting down at the children in the stern cabin. "Be quiet, you noisy brats. I can't understand you, and maybe you don't know what I am saying, but if you don't stop whining, I will throw you all overboard."

Susan prodded her brother. "Get up, William. We have to go take care of the children."

The pirates watched with great interest and growing amazement as Susan and William fed the children, led them in morning devotions and kept them busy throughout the day. They could not understand why these two children commanded the respect of all the rest or how Susan could calm a crying little one with a touch and a word. She smiled to herself when she overheard them referring to her as "Little Miss Angel."

Whenever Susan and William were not busy, they looked anxiously toward the shore, hoping to see Harold and the others returning. It was suppertime and they were handing tins of spaghetti and peaches down into the stern cabin when a rowboat bumped into the side of the boat. Harold's excited voice preceded him up the rope ladder.

"Susan! William! I'm back. Everything is going to be all right." His head popped above the railing as he continued talking. "We are all going ashore for a couple of days until they can get a ship ready to go with us. They are going to help us capture Hagen."

Quickly Harold told his friends about his meeting the night before with the council of the elders and about their final decision that afternoon. By the time supper was over other boats had arrived to take everyone ashore. William was last in line to climb down the rope ladder. As Susan looked up she saw one foot appear over the railing and then disappear. A few moments later William stuck his head over and called out, "Catch." Down came the atlas with Susan's makeshift protractor inside. Seconds later William dropped into the boat, and they headed toward the little pirate village.

The next two days provided a wonderful change of pace from

life aboard boat. At first Harold, Susan, and William worried about how the other children would manage, since they could not speak the Mother Tongue. The children of the village, however, were delighted to have so many new playmates, and tag or hide and seek can be played as well with smiles and laughter as with words.

Occasionally the three leaders played with the rest of the children or translated for them when there was a major misunderstanding, but most of their time was spent with the council and the captains, who were planning the expedition. The men were fascinated by the atlas, for they had never seen such an accurate picture of their coastline before. They made careful tracings from the maps of British Columbia, Washington, Oregon, California and Baja California. They were also delighted by Susan's protractor and made several wooden copies of that.

The children also had questions of their own, and surprisingly one of their best sources of information was the pirate captain, who had become quite friendly. William nicknamed him P. C. (short for Pirate Captain). When William explained what the English letters meant, he accepted the label with a laugh. On the second evening ashore the children and their pirate friend were sitting on the beach looking toward the ships at anchor. "P. C.," asked William, "why does our boat have one triangular sail, while the large ships of your village have square sails?"

"Bring me your atlas," answered P. C. "Every ship builder up and down the coast has his favorite style. I can tell you the maker of every craft that sails these waters. Yours was made by a colony up here." He pointed to the mouth of the Columbia River between Oregon and Washington. "What puzzles me is how this man you call Hagen managed to have it delivered to the Great Bay." He pointed to San Francisco." I have been there, but I would not want to live so close to the gates between our worlds. I know where the southern gates are also, near the place you call El Rosario, and no one lives there either."

Early on the third morning after their arrival, the children were rowed back out to their boat. Following P. C.'s ship, they left the harbor of Santa Cruz Island and headed southeast along the coast. P. C. had insisted on leading the expedition. "If I am going to give up piracy," he said, "this may be my last chance for a big adventure. I'll capture this Hagen for you, and I hope he puts up a good fight!"

This leg of the journey was very pleasant. The skies were clear, and the children felt safe. Two of P. C.'s sailors were aboard, and even though they could not speak a common language, they were able to teach Pete and Al quite a bit about sailing. In order not to become separated, the ships anchored close to shore every night. Toward the middle of the seventh day P. C. signaled for them to sail closer. When they were near enough, he shouted across the water, "The place where you are supposed to meet Hagen is around the next point. We will anchor here now, and tonight my men and I will go ashore. Tomorrow morning, take your boat to the rendezvous and wait for Hagen. He may already be there, but let us capture him before you land."

The next morning shortly after dawn, Pete and Al hoisted the sail, weighed anchor and sailed slowly around the point. There on the shore were the two great piles of rocks that Siegfriend had drawn for them. They anchored and scanned the beach and the surrounding hills with the binoculars. P. C. and his sailors were well hidden and nothing moved on the beach except a few sandpipers.

"I half expected Hagen to be waiting for us," said Susan. "We ve taken much longer to get here than he expected. I guess e is nothing to do but wait."

And wait they did. The morning hours dragged on and on. Lunchtime came and went, and the children stopped staring over the railing toward the shore. About four thirty Al woke them all up from an afternoon siesta. "Susan, Harold, William. I see someone coming over the hill, but it doesn't look like Hagen."

William reached Al first and took the binoculars he offered. "Hey, Susan! It's not Hagen. It's Dad!" William began jumping, shouting and waving, but his father was too far away to see or hear.

Susan took the next turn with the binoculars, but as she watched she cried out, "Oh no! P. C. thinks he is Hagen. They have surrounded him with bows and arrows and drawn swords. Now they have him gagged so he can't use the Mother Tongue. Now they are tying him up. Al, Pete. Will you take William and me ashore right away?"

"Yes, Miss," answered Pete as he headed toward the stern to pull in the dinghy.

P. C. met them at the shore. Mr. Struthers was lying in the sand further up on the beach, bound hand and foot and surrounded by armed sailors. "Well, I got your man for you, but it was not any fun. He didn't even put up a fight. Hey, I have an idea! How about if we untie him and let him fight me. I'll give him a sword, and if he beats me, he can go free. Don't worry, though. He won't win. I am the best that there is, and I'll have him skewered within two minutes."

"No, P. C.," said William. "We do not want you to skewer him. That man is not Hagen. He is our dad."

"Oh," said P. C., looking very dejected. "Well, I guess we will have to untie him and let him go without a fight," which they did.

Susan, William and their dad all clung to each other and wept for joy. Finally they broke apart and Susan asked, "Where is Hagen? Is everything all right?"

"Yes," answered Mr. Struthers, "but it almost wasn't. After you helped Andrea to escape from Earth-Two back into San Francisco, she went to the hotel and discovered that Joe was her dad. She was afraid to stay in San Francisco, so she talked her dad into leaving before the Wilsons arrived. They wrote Mr. and Mrs. Wilson a note and left it on a bed in the hotel room, but the wind must have blown it away. When you did not show up to greet the Wilsons at the dock they wondered where you were. When you were not at the hotel room, and did not show up all afternoon they began to worry. That evening, however, Joe and Andrea came back because they felt guilty about running away. So the Wilsons called us, and we phoned an Earth-Two ranger who lives in Greece. He entered Earth-Two and to tell Ulysses and Frigga. They flew to the States, and we all came down to El Rosario together. Ulysses and Frigga captured Hagen a few days ago, and Ulysses has taken him back to Greece for a trial before the Ruling Council of Earth-Two. Frigga and the rest are still in El Rosario. One of us has been coming through the entrance vortex every afternoon to look for your boat while the others wait by the exit. So here I am. If I don't show up pretty soon, they will send Frigga in after me. Are you ready to go home?"

They were, but it was after dark by the time they got all of the children ashore and up to the exit. By then Frigga had indeed arrived. Harold, Susan, and William threw their arms around her and kissed her. Her eyes were shining with pleasure as she said, "I am very proud of you. I could never ask for a better reward for teaching you than to have you do such a thing as this."

Then she turned to P. C. and his men. "Thank you for your ɔ. I understand you were somewhat disappointed that Sam hers was not Hagen, but I will speak to Ulysses, the man you call the Wanderer, on your behalf. He had already heard rumors of piracy on this coast, and he planned to investigate it sometime soon. When he comes, he will be glad that you have forsaken your evil ways. The children say that you like adventure; perhaps Ulysses will be able to use you as a deputy. Would that please you?"

"Yes, Miss Frigga. It would indeed," replied P. C. He stood up a little straighter and thrust out his chest.

"One more thing, P.C. Will you please return the children's boat to San Francisco Bay—the Great Bay? Ulysses was quite disturbed about some unanswered questions in this case, and I have a feeling the boat may be of use if it is anchored there. The children can tell you where to leave it."

"Yes, again, Miss Frigga. You can count on me."

Harold, Susan, and William spent a few minutes with P.C. and then said goodbye to him and his men. As the sailors turned away and walked back toward their ship, four adults and twenty-seven children disappeared from Earth-Two.

After the hugs and tears and happy greetings were all over in Earth-One, Mrs. Wilson held her son at arm's length and said, "Harold, I know it has only been a couple of weeks, but you seem to have grown somehow. You are almost a man."

Pete turned to her and said, "He's better than most men, Ma'am." Then, speaking to Harold, he said, "Captain, if you ever need crewmen for another voyage, you can count on me.

APPENDIX 1—EXPERIMENT ON THE PLANE

If you want to repeat Mr. Wilson's experiment on the plane (Chapter 1) first cut a cardboard rectangle of some convenient size (4 inches by 6 inches would do). Then place marks as shown on the diagram and number them (see the next page). The marks should be the same distance apart (for example ¼ inch). Tape a string to the middle of the back and bring it over the top to dangle down in front. Tie a small weight to the bottom. When the plane is about to take off, hold the cardboard so that the string hangs straight down through the zero. Brace yourself so that you can hold it steady when the plane takes off. As soon as the plane begins to accelerate, the string will move backward. The string may not stay in exactly one place, but make your best guess at the average spot where it crosses the bottom set of numbers. Ask someone else with a watch to measure the length of time the plane accelerates down the runway until it takes off. If you ever have an opportunity to take a wonderful course called physics, you will find out what the formulas below mean and why they work. Until then, just have fun.

T = length of time the plane is accelerating down the runway (in seconds)
H = the number of marks in the vertical direction (in this case 16)
L = the number where the string crosses the bottom of the cardboard (in this case 3.5.)

From these 3 measurements you can determine the following:

A = acceleration of the plane = (L/H) x 32 [L divided by H, times 32]
S = speed of the plane at takeoff (in feet per second) = A x T [A times T]
D = distance down the runway the plane traveled before takeoff [in feet]
= ½ x A x T² [½ times A times T times T]

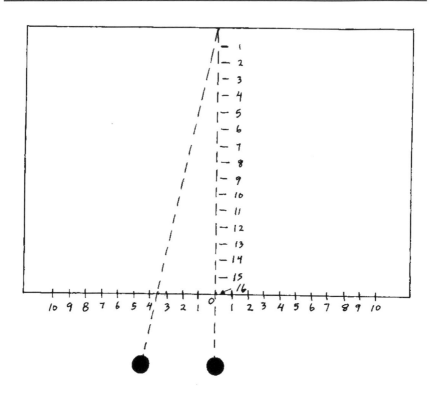

Mr. Wilson's homemade device for his experiment on the plane

APPENDIX 2—MEASURING YOUR LATITUDE

I f you want to measure your latitude with an instrument like the one Susan made (Chapter 7), first find a protractor. Glue or tape a straw along the top edge and tape a string through the center of the zero line. Sight through the straw at the North Star and have a friend notice where the string crosses the circle. Be sure you are looking at the set of numbers that count down from 90°. (Some protractors have more than one set of numbers.)

Your latitude will be 90° minus the second number. In the case of the illustration below the latitude would be 90° − 50° = 40°. Do the experiment several times and average your results. Check your answer with a map and see how close you are to the correct value.

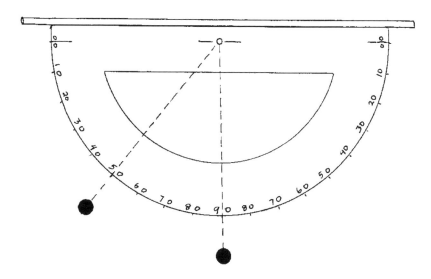

The Village

The Higgledy-
Piggledy House

CHAPTER 1--A BIG SURPRISE

"Hi, Harold. Mind if I join you?" Frigga's head popped above the floor of the tree house. "Your Mom said I would find you here. She also said that you were pretty grumpy when you came home from school."

Harold nodded as Frigga climbed up and sat down beside him. Usually her bright smile and happy blue eyes cheered him and made him feel warm and special, but not today.

"What's wrong, Harold?" she asked. "Will you please tell me?"

Harold hung his head and sighed. "I know I shouldn't complain, but ever since we came back from rescuing those children, I have not had one minute to myself. It was bad enough that Susan, William and I had to make up all the schoolwork we missed, but then you started pushing us twice as hard as you ever did before. When we come home from school, we have to run, do push-ups and sit-ups, and climb ropes. After supper you have us memorizing vocabulary and learning how to focus our minds by using the Mother Tongue. I have not watched one TV show in the last month, and when I go to bed, I'm so tired I can't even read any of my favorite books."

Harold paused, took a deep breath, and then hurried on. "I know that you love us, and you keep telling us how proud you are of us, but I don't think you could be any harder on us if you were angry at us."

"Sometimes people say that about God too, Harold, but whenever our Heavenly Father puts us through hard times, He always has a good reason. And so do I."

Frigga leaned over and gently brushed the boy's cheek with one finger. He looked up at her, basking in the warmth of her affection. Finally, he said, "Thanks. I feel better. What do you have in mind for us today?"

"Anything you like, Harold. I will have a special surprise for all three of you later on, but for this afternoon you are free. What do you want to do? Would you like to go off by yourself?"

"No," replied Harold slowly. "I want to be with you, but can we do something that is fun and quiet?"

"Sure, Harold. How about reading one of your favorite books together?"

"That is a great idea, Frigga! Actually, I have a new book my Dad bought me when he was away on his last business trip. I'll go see if Susan and William want to join us."

So it was that three happy children flopped across Harold's bed as Frigga turned to page one and read,

In a hole in the ground there lived a hobbit. Not a nasty, dirty, wet hole, filled with the ends of worms and an oozy smell, nor yet a dry, bare, sandy hole with nothing in it to sit down on or to eat: it was a hobbit-hole, and that means comfort.[3]

An hour and a half later Frigga laid down the book and said, "Time for supper and your surprise. We are all eating over at the Struthers's house tonight, so go wash up. I'll meet you there in a few minutes." Throughout the afternoon she had steadfastly refused to give any hint of what was ahead. After most of their guesses she simply smiled, but when William, in desperation, asked if it was a pet purple panda, she laughed merrily and scrubbed his tousled hair with her fist. None of the children even came close to guessing the guest who was waiting for them.

After washing, they walked across the lawn that separated their two houses, chattering happily about hobbits and dwarves

---

[3] This is the opening paragraph of a perfectly delightful story called *The Hobbit* by J. R. R. Tolkien.

and dragons. As the kitchen door opened in front of them, Susan looked up and shouted, "Ulysses! Are you our surprise?"

"Well, I suppose I am at least a part of it." Ulysses chuckled. "Come here, and let me have a look at all of you."

The children stood shyly before the tall ranger, waiting for him to finish his inspection. Although he was their friend, they felt as if they were in the presence of a legend or the mysterious hero out of some ancient saga. Their eyes took in his high leather boots, his forest-green clothing and the color-shifting cape clasped at the throat by a gold medallion. The face above the medallion was smiling.

"I have not seen you since before Christmas, and just look at how you have grown. Frigga tells me that you are making wonderful progress in your training. I am counting on that."

The children wondered what he meant, but before they could ask, Mrs. Struthers called them in to supper. Frigga came in right behind them; she, too, was dressed as a ranger. Susan looked at Harold and raised her eyebrows in a question. Harold just shrugged and shook his head.

At the dinner table roast beef, mashed potatoes and gravy, snow peas and finally strawberry pie occupied most of their attention for the better part of an hour. Finally, Ulysses pushed back his chair and said, "Harold, Susan, William—I have come to ask for your help. If you wonder why Frigga has been pushing you so hard (he looked at Harold), the answer is that she has been training you for a special mission. I wanted to take you away with me tomorrow, but some people (he looked at Mrs. Struthers and Mrs. Wilson) insisted that you finish out the school year."

Susan and Harold, who still had pie in their mouths, stopped chewing. William, whose mouth was empty, burst out, "A mission? You need our help? Where will we be going? What are we supposed to do? Will it be dangerous?"

Ulysses laughed. "Questions, questions, questions. You may have grown, William, but you certainly have not changed. Let me see. Where should I begin?"

Ulysses sat still for a moment; the smile faded from his lips, and when he spoke, the cheery twinkle had gone from his eyes. "I am worried about Hagen. When I first heard about his plan to capture children and sell them to Asian slave traders, several points bothered me. I wondered how he had accomplished so much in such a short time. How did he learn English? How did he find his way to the San Francisco vortex? How did he gain control of the shop where the vortex was located? (It used to be held by one of our people.) How did he acquire an Earth-Two sailboat and set up his operation?"

"Questions, questions, questions," whispered William with a grin.

"Shh!" said his father. "Don't interrupt."

Ulysses smiled briefly and continued, "After Frigga and I captured Hagen, I took him for trial before Earth-Two's Ruling Council. I thought the Council might want you children to come as witnesses, but Hagen did not even bother to deny the charges I brought against him. Next, I assumed that the Elders would pass sentence immediately, but again I was wrong. After the initial hearing, Hagen was kept in custody, but not in prison. He was treated almost as a guest. Then I learned of secret meetings between him and some of the Council members. My informants knew he had been taken late at night to the private chambers of certain Elders, but they could never find out which ones. Something is very, very wrong."

When he paused, Frigga stepped in. "Hagen could be quite charming and persuasive when he wanted to be," she said. "When he came to our village and recruited me for his cause, he made it sound so noble. We would heal the centuries-old breach between Earth-One and Earth-Two. Our knowledge of the Mother Tongue combined with your world's great advances in science would usher in a golden age of peace and prosperity. That is what he said. I was taken in. I thought he was a hero, but when I saw how cruelly he treated you, I realized that his golden dreams were just a cover for his own selfish ambition.

"There are other people in Earth-Two who think like that. Most of them are not as cruel and selfish as Hagen is, but they do not have the patience to wait for God to bring our two worlds together. Ulysses and I, along with many others, believe the reunion will come about when Jesus returns. Perhaps the prophecies of a little child leading the beasts will come true when the Mother Tongue is restored to Earth-One. If that is the case, then we must simply wait for God to act."

"Yes," said Mr. Struthers. "That's what we believe, too. Jesus warned us not to believe false prophets who would predict the time of His return. How sad and foolish that so many people, both in Earth-One and Earth-Two, think that they know when Christ will come back again!"

Frigga sighed. "It is even worse when people try to bring in the kingdom of God by some act of evil. That is what Ulysses fears. He thinks Hagen has found an ally on the Ruling Council, someone who is helping him now and who may have helped him in the past. This elder may believe kidnapping, murder, or other crimes are all right if they help to establish the future kingdom of peace."

Ulysses nodded. "The Council praised me for capturing Hagen and then dismissed me. They said I was needed in my own territory, but I felt sure that they were trying to get rid of me. I think someone knew I was suspicious. So here I am, back on the job, but I left my eyes and my ears behind."

William opened his mouth, but before he could ask, Ulysses chuckled and said, "Friends, William. My eyes and ears are my friends. A mouse will not enter or leave Hagen's room without my knowing of it. Now we come to your part. Harold, Susan, William—I need more eyes and ears. I believe that the answer to my questions may lie in the Earth-Two village where your sailboat was made. I want to send you there this summer as spies. Frigga will tell you that persuading your parents to let you go was no easy task, but they have finally given in. If you are willing, she will take you back to San Francisco where you will pick up your sailboat. I am glad she had the forethought to ask P. C. to deliver it there. Your friends Al and Pete have agreed to go along as sailors. I understand that they are taking a course in navigation this spring.

"Frigga will not be staying with you because I think the villagers are more likely to talk freely to children than to a full-fledged ranger. She will be visiting settlements to the north of the village. I plan to come up the coast from the south because I have long intended to do that anyway. Perhaps Frigga and I will be able to discover clues in other villages that will help us solve our mystery. If I can find P.C., and if he is willing to help me, I should be able to meet you and Frigga at the village in August."

Ulysses paused, looked deeply into the eyes of each child in turn, and then said, "Your mission may be dangerous. Are you willing to go?"

Harold looked first at Susan, then at William. He read the answer in their faces before he heard them in his mind. Then he answered for all three of them. "Yes, Sir. We are honored and thrilled to be asked."

William opened his mouth but before he could speak, Ulysses said, "You have questions, right, William?" William nodded. "There will be plenty of time for that later. You can badger Frigga every day until you leave, but now I have presents for you. From a large bag behind his chair he pulled three bundles wrapped in brown paper and tied up with string. "These are your traveling outfits. Go put them on."

Ten minutes later three small and very excited rangers walked back through the door of the dining room. They were dressed in forest-green trousers and shirts with tall leather boots. Over their shoulders were draped color-shifting capes, clasped at the neck with silver medallions.

Frigga looked at them pleasure glowing in her eyes. "You are to be rangers-in-training this summer. That will help to explain your presence to the villagers. I will ask them to teach you as much about life in Earth-Two as you can absorb. I hope that in several years you will pass the test and become rangers indeed. You have worked so hard and learned so much already. Your parents and I are very proud of you."

Mr. Wilson and Mr. Struthers were ready with their cameras, so the children posed together, then with Frigga and Ulysses, then for individual photos, then for photos with their parents. (Both fathers were severely afflicted with camera-itis.)

Finally, Ulysses brought the evening to a close. "You men must have enough pictures for two scrapbooks apiece. Children, I want you to have a good night's rest. If you thought Frigga was pushing you hard, just wait until tomorrow. We have some very special lessons to teach you, and I promise to work you harder than you have ever been worked before. Good night."

CHAPTER 2—A NEW SKILL

"Time to get up, Susan." It was her mother's voice and knock. "No it isn't. It's still dark outside." Susan rolled away from the window and put the pillow over her head.

"Have you forgotten? Ulysses wants you up and dressed and fed and out of the house by six o'clock."

Ulysses! Susan's eyes popped open as memories of the night before poured into her waking thoughts. It was Friday, but they were not going to school. Ulysses planned to give them two full days of training before he left to make final preparations for their mission. She was out of bed and pulling on the green top of her new ranger's outfit when she remembered what that meant. "Ugh! One more day of school work to make up!" she muttered. Susan liked school, but she hated catching up to the class on her own, so she usually insisted on going even when she did not feel well.

Her father and William were already waiting at the breakfast table when she came downstairs. Susan's mouth twitched into a brief frown. As usual William had not bothered to comb his hair. Mrs. Struthers sat down while her husband asked God's blessing on the food and their day, then she got up to serve pancakes, sausages, and eggs. "No cold cereal today," she announced. "Ulysses said you need something that will stick to your ribs."

After breakfast Susan and William shouldered their school backpacks. This time, of course, they held no books, only large lunches. Ulysses, Frigga and Harold met them in the yard, and the group headed toward the vortex in the wilderness behind their houses. Ulysses wanted to conduct their lessons in Earth-Two where there would be no possibility of interruption.

The children were in excellent physical condition, so they had no trouble keeping up with the quick pace set by Ulysses. As they walked, he explained what he had in mind. "I have come to teach you a new skill, one that is known to the rangers and the Ruling Council and only a few others in Earth-Two. I want you to learn how to talk to each other and to Frigga and me with your minds instead of your mouths."

"Wow! Does that mean we will be like the mind reader we saw at the circus?" asked William.

"Absolutely not!" snapped Ulysses. "Mind readers are all fakes who use tricks to make people think they can read minds. Unfortunately people like that sometimes get religion. A few years ago in your country a reporter investigated a so-called faith healer who claimed to be getting divine revelations about the sicknesses of people in his meetings. It turned out that someone was transmitting the information to him through a radio receiver plugged into his ear. I know that God can give us special insight into the needs of others, but religious quacks like that one make me mad."

"No one can really read minds," added Frigga. "When you learn how to talk to each other with your minds, you will see it is just like talking on a telephone. You cannot hear what the other person is thinking, only what he is saying."

"Why aren't you teaching us yourself, Frigga," asked Susan. "I am very glad Ulysses is here, but did he need to come?"

"There are two reasons, Susan," replied Frigga. "First, this is all rather new to me, so Ulysses will do a better job of teaching you. Almost everything I have taught you for the past few weeks was leading up to this, but I wanted him to come for the final lessons. The second reason is that you cannot learn to talk to anyone far away unless you do it face to face the first time, so if you want to talk to Ulysses, you will have to spend some time with him."

"Are you going to teach our parents so that we can talk to them while we are away this summer," asked Harold?

"No," said Ulysses. "Mind-talk will not work between the worlds, only within one world. You may try to teach your parents if you like. It will be good practice for you, but I am not sure they will be able to learn. The younger you are the easier this skill is to master, but older people can sometimes do it if they have been well trained in other uses of the Mother Tongue. Frigga is an exceptional student. I have never taught anyone of any age who learned so quickly."

In a short while the little group stood atop the vortex hill at the head of the canyon. Frigga spoke one word in the Mother Tongue that sounded almost like the Sanskrit word, antaH.[4] The world began to spin around them, and the children closed their eyes for a few seconds. When they opened them again, they were surrounded by the tall, uncut trees of Earth-Two. They walked down the hill to a grassy meadow beside the stream that flowed out from the canyon wall. There they sat down while Ulysses explained what they would be doing.

"I will work with you one at a time. We will hold hands and repeat together a long sequence of words in the Mother Tongue. There is a kind of rhythm in these words, and as we say them our minds will begin to move together, like people marching in time to the same music. We will need to go through this sequence several times, the first few times out loud, then whispering, and finally in our minds. When our minds are locked into the same rhythm, we will be able to talk to each other without making any sounds. After I have finished with you, then you will go through the same process with Frigga and finally with each other. It will be a little easier each time, but

---

[4] See *The Vortex*, Chapter 4, for the significance of this word. It is pronounced *untuh*, with heavy breathing out on the final *h*.

you will find it very tiring. I think I will start with William."

Susan and Harold sat quietly and watched as Ulysses began teaching William what to say. The words were all part of their vocabulary lessons from the preceding weeks, so the chant was not just a series of meaningless sounds like abracadabra. It was more like a song or poem.

After William and Ulysses had chanted the sequence several times, they fell silent, staring into each other's eyes. A few minutes later Ulysses released his hands, and William walked to the other side of the clearing. He closed his eyes and put his hands over his ears. After a few moments he turned toward Susan and Harold and exclaimed, "Wow! It is hard to believe that Ulysses has not been talking out loud. Even with my hands over my ears it sounded as if we were still face to face. He says you are next, Susan."

As Susan walked over to take her place in front of Ulysses, William began rummaging in his backpack. "I'm starved. Hey, Frigga, is it all right if I take a nap before my session with you."

"Sure, William," she replied, "a short one anyway."

William ate and slept for perhaps thirty minutes while Harold played in the creek. Shortly after William began working with Frigga, it was Harold's turn to be taught by Ulysses. Susan, seeing that Frigga was still occupied, curled up without eating and immediately fell asleep. Frigga woke her before she was ready to get up, and as the day progressed, she became increasingly tired. So did William and Harold.

The sun was setting by the time the children had learned to mind-talk with each other, and they were so exhausted they could hardly stand up. On the trip back to the exit vortex, Ulysses and Frigga held their hands to keep them from stumbling. Later on all three of them fell asleep at the dinner table, so their fathers carried them up to bed.

* * * *

"Time to get up, Susan." It was Frigga's voice instead of her mother's.

"No it isn't. It's still dark outside." Susan rolled away from the window and put the pillow over her head.

"Have you forgotten? Ulysses wants you up and dressed and fed and out of the house by six o'clock."

"Okay! Okay! I'm getting up, Frigga." Susan opened her eyes, switched on the bedside lamp and looked around. The door to her room was still shut. "Frigga, where are you?" (This time Susan spoke in her mind, not with her lips.)

"I'm over at the Wilsons' house. I told your mother I would surprise you this morning. See you in a few minutes. I have to call William next."

This time Susan beat William to the breakfast table. "Frigga must have given me a few minutes' head start," she thought.

In spite of the fact that this was Saturday, her mother and father were both up to see the children off. "Are you feeling all right, Susan?" her father asked. "I was worried about you last night. I told Ulysses he was pushing you too hard, but he said it was necessary."

"Yes, I'm fine, Dad, but I wish I could sleep until noon. Mind-talk is great. Ulysses said we could try to teach you and Mom, but he did not think you would be able to learn it."

"Yes, I know, honey. Here's William. Time to pray."

Susan's father asked God's blessing on the food and on the day, and then his heart seemed to overflow and spill out of his mouth as he prayed fervently for strength and protection for Susan and William. By the time he was finished Susan's eyes were moist. It meant so much to hear her father praying earnestly on her behalf.

After breakfast the little group of teachers and pupils walked up the canyon and again entered Earth-Two. The lesson this day was different, but no less tiring. Ulysses laid his hands on each child's head in turn and mind-talked at super speed. Thus, he was able to teach them in an hour's time what would normally have taken several months to learn. Frigga did not help with this project. On two occasions Ulysses had taught her using this method, but she was not yet ready to teach others.

Ulysses gave each of them two lessons, with food and a rest in between. On the way home, William said, "I have a question. I'm almost too tired even to think, but I want to ask anyway."

Ulysses laughed. "Go ahead, William," he said.

"Everything happened so fast that I'm not sure exactly what you put into my head. I think it was mostly Mother-Tongue vocabulary and Earth-Two history, and maybe some ways of defending myself. Can you teach me all of the stuff I am supposed to learn at school, so I don't have to go anymore? Or if I do have to go, I could get an A on all of the tests without studying."

"I was waiting for that question," chuckled Ulysses. "Maybe I could teach you, but I am not going to do it. In the first place, you can only absorb a certain number of facts at one time. If I kept up that pace for a week, it would damage your mind. In the second place, you need to learn the discipline of study. That is one of the most important lessons you can get from school. Discipline in your studies and in your physical exercise can help you to learn the spiritual disciplines that really matter. As the apostle Paul wrote to Timothy, 'But have nothing to do with worldly fables fit only for old women. On the other hand, discipline yourself for the purpose of godliness; for bodily discipline is only of little profit, but godliness is profitable for all things, since it holds promise for the present life and also for the life to come' (1 Timothy 4:7-8). I do not want you to become physically or mentally lazy, and most of all I do not want you to become spiritually lazy."

"I was afraid you were going to say something like that,"

sighed William. Then he smiled as he remembered what he used to think. When he was younger, he thought self-discipline meant spanking yourself. Now he knew it just meant lots of hard work. Little did he know how much would depend on his disciplined study that summer.

CHAPTER 3—A NEW TRICK

"Psst! Susan, wake up!" This time it was the voice of Ulysses. Her eyes popped open, and she straightened up. She glanced down at the other end of her pew past her parents and William to where Ulysses was sitting. Apparently no one else had heard him, so it must have been mind-talk.

Susan loved her pastor and she usually understood most of his sermon, but this morning she was still very tired from the lessons of the past two days. "I'm glad the Lord gave us a day to rest," she thought. "Otherwise we probably would never find time to worship Him." In an effort to figure out what the message was all about she leaned over to look at her mother's sermon notes. Her own notes stopped after the pastor's first point, but her mother was jotting down key words under his third major heading.

Pastor Smith was saying something about the Christian's calling in life, but Susan was not sure what he meant, so she turned in her Bible to the verses listed for that part of the sermon. "Only, as the Lord has assigned to each one, as God has called each, in this manner let him walk. And so I direct in all the churches . . .. Were you called while a slave? Do not worry about it; but if you are able also to be free, rather do that. For he who was called in the Lord while a slave, is the Lord's freedman; likewise he who was called while free, is Christ's slave" (1 Corinthians 7:17, 21-22). Susan was still puzzling over the passage when the pastor finished his sermon and led them in the final hymn, so she decided to ask her father about the message over dinner.

After church, people stood around and talked for a while. Most of them had not met Ulysses, so he had to be introduced to everyone. He looked very distinguished in his charcoal gray suit, and one of the unmarried ladies finally backed him into a corner in order to have him to herself. He looked as if he wanted to escape, but no one seemed inclined to go to his rescue. Frigga and Mrs. Struthers were trying very hard not to laugh out loud.

Harold, Susan, and William drifted outside to sit in the sun and talk with their friends. When he saw them, Jimmy Sanders left the group of boys playing basketball and walked over. Brittany, who had a crush on Jimmy, followed close behind. "Summer vacation is just three weeks away, so what are you guys planning to do?" he asked.

"Our friend, Frigga, is taking us to a primitive village on the West Coast," replied Harold. "There we will learn what it is like to live for a summer without all conveniences of modern civilization."

"What do you mean by 'primitive,' Harold? Which modern conveniences will you have to do without?" Brittany wrinkled up her nose in disgust as she spoke.

"Well, I guess the main thing is that there will be no electricity. That means no TV, no computer games, not even any electric lights. There will be no running water in the houses, no indoor toilets, no MacDonalds and probably no place to shop, except maybe one general store or a farmers' market on Saturday."

"But you can get away, can't you?" asked Brittany. She was obviously horrified at the prospect of being stuck in such a place. "I mean, can't you take a bus to the mall at least once a week?"

"There is no mall, Brittany," laughed Susan, "and if there were, we would have to walk or maybe paddle a canoe to get there."

"That sounds pretty neat," said Jimmy. He looked pointedly

at Brittany, who immediately stomped off. "Do you suppose I could come with you?"

"No, I'm afraid not," replied Harold. "The village isn't on any map; the trip is part of Frigga's training program for us. She makes us work pretty hard, but we are learning quite a bit about wilderness survival and, uh. . . well, other things."

"Do you suppose my parents could hire her to teach me too?" asked Jimmy.

"No, Jimmy," said Frigga, who had just come up behind him. "You are a fine young man, and it would be a pleasure to teach you, but my services are not for hire. The Wilsons and the Strutherses do not pay me anything. I am training Harold, Susan, and William because it is part of my calling—just as Pastor Smith was saying this morning. Ulysses, who is my teacher and my boss, asked me to take on this assignment because he believes God has an unusual calling in store for Harold, Susan, and William."

"I'm afraid I missed some of the pastor's message this morning, Frigga," said Susan. "I dozed off in the middle of it. I didn't understand the part about calling. I have heard of Christians being called by God to become missionaries, but don't think that is what he was talking about."

"I was awake," piped up William, with smirk on his face. "Pastor Smith said that every Christian has a calling from God. Your calling is the place where God puts you. Right now you and I are called by God to be obedient children. Dad has a calling to work and to take care of Mom and us. If we are faithful and work hard at our callings, we can please God just as much as missionaries and pastors do."

"That is right," said Frigga. "But, William, I was sitting behind you, and if I remember correctly, the only reason you were awake is that your dad kept prodding you."

William hung his head and said, "I'm sorry, Susan. I guess

we were both pretty tired."

"Maybe you two and Harold should all take a nap after dinner," suggested Frigga. Then turning to Jimmy she said, "I know you are disappointed that you cannot have the same training as these three, but I think God has a very special calling for you. I can see His hand at work in you already, and I am eager to see what He will do with you in the days ahead. When He gives you your life's work, you will discover it is exactly right for you. Just stick close to Him every day. That is the secret of being where He wants you in the future."

Frigga placed her hand briefly on Jimmy's head, and gave him one of her extra special smiles. Her blue eyes looked deeply into his, and Jimmy went home with a happy heart and a great determination not to disappoint her.

The children did not go to bed that afternoon, but they did doze off and on as they listened to the grownups talk in the Strutherses' living room. By the next morning Ulysses was gone, and that afternoon Frigga picked up their training again. Their schedule, however, was much lighter than before. They practiced mind-talk, which was fairly easy when they were close to each other and much more tiring over long distances. Frigga also began teaching them new skills. One of the most useful was the ability to fall quickly into a deep sleep and yet to wake up instantly at the slightest hint of danger.

On the second Saturday after Ulysses left, the children had the whole day to themselves. Frigga and their parents attended the funeral of one of the older church members, and they had all promised to help serve the dinner and clean up afterwards.

William was sitting in their tree house, and Susan was trying to see her reflection in the old well when Harold joined them. "I have been thinking about our mind-talk," he said. "Why does it only work between two people at a time? When I am talking to Susan, William can't hear us. When I am talking to William,

Susan is left out. I wonder if we can learn to include all three of us in the same conversation. I have an idea. Are you willing to go to Earth-Two to try it out?"

Susan and William were not only willing; they were excited. Within fifteen minutes they had scrounged up food for snacks and lunch and were on their way up into the canyon. Susan left a note for her parents. It said, "Gone to Earth-Two. Back for supper. Love, Susan."

"My idea is this," said Harold once they had passed through the vortex. "All three of us will hold hands and repeat the mind-talk chant together. We will try to lock all three of our minds into the same rhythm." Susan and William nodded, and they began the experiment. They found, however, that it was much more difficult to link three minds than two. One of them always seemed to be a split-second ahead of or behind the others.

When, after an hour, they had made no progress, Harold let go and dropped his hands into his lap. "I guess it was a dumb idea after all," he sighed.

"No, it is not a dumb idea," answered Susan. "I still think it might work. Let's have a snack and a rest and try again." So they did, but they still had no better success.

Harold and William were tired and ready to give up, but Susan persisted. "William, you remember what Grandpa used to say: 'If at first you don't succeed—try second base and shortstop.'"

"What does that mean?" asked Harold.

"It means," replied William, "that Susan is not going to let us stop until we try at least one more time."

So the three children sat down together in the green meadow with the blue sky overhead. An hour passed, and William tried to let go, but Susan held on. After an hour and a half, Harold started to stand up, but Susan pulled him down. At the two-hour mark, their legs and their minds were numb, but by now the rhythm of the chant had become almost automatic. The was no longer any conscious effort at remembering and saying the words, but still the chant surged on and on, like a song you can't get out of your head. The words seemed to take on a life of their own, and suddenly they all realized together that their minds had been linked for the past several minutes.

William hopped up and down with excitement; Susan cried softly with relief and joy; Harold just lay back in the grass and looked up at the sky. Sometime later, after the last of their food and a rest, three very satisfied children headed back home for supper.

"Are we going to tell Frigga," asked William?

"Of course we are," answered his sister, "but we don't need to tell her right away. Let's see if she guesses our secret on her own."

* * * *

Several days later Frigga was mind-talking to Ulysses, who was preparing to enter a southwestern vortex for his trip up Earth-Two's California coast. "Ulysses, is it possible for three people to enter into the same mind-talk conversation?"

"It has often been attempted, Frigga, but I don't know of anyone who has ever succeeded. Why do you ask?"

"Oh, I suppose it is just my imagination, but the children do make me wonder sometimes."

CHAPTER 4—A MEETING OF FRIENDS

The last week of school seemed to drag on forever, but finally the day for their departure was at hand. Mrs. Struthers and Mrs. Wilson had fussed and fretted over all the little details of the trip. Did the children have enough underwear and socks? How about tooth brushes and soap and clothing for cold weather and books and flashlights and batteries and on and on. In the end, however, Frigga only allowed one hiking knapsack for each of them. They were going to spend the summer in an Earth-Two village, and she wanted them to live as the villagers did.

As he stood in line at the airport waiting to pass through the metal detector, Harold was filled with an expectation of high adventure. Something big was waiting for them; he could feel it, and he shivered all over with excitement. He looked over at Susan who appeared quiet and thoughtful, then at William who was trying to keep his balance as he hopped up and down on one foot with his eyes closed. His mom and Mrs. Struthers were trying hard not to cry, but they could not help sniffling into a Kleenex occasionally. Mr. Struthers was staring out the window at their plane, his lips moving in a silent prayer. Harold's dad opened his mouth as if he were about to launch into one final lecture about being careful. At that moment Frigga's voice broke into Harold's reverie.

"Come on, Harold. Pay attention. It is our turn."

Frigga and the three children passed through the metal detector and then turned to wave goodbye and blow kisses at their parents. Forty-five minutes later they boarded the plane, and five hours after that they landed in San Francisco. Pete and Al were waiting at the gate for them.

"Hello, Captain," said Pete to Harold. "Al and I are looking forward to sailing under you again. Hello, Susan. Hello, William." The men shook hands with the boys; Susan gave each of them a hug.

"Hello, Miss Frigga," said both men in unison. Although they had met her only once before, they seemed to think she was a very special person, and they treated her with great respect.

"Do you want us go get your baggage, Miss," asked Al?

"No, Al, but thank you. All we have are these knapsacks, which we kept with us on the plane. I would like to go straight to the shop in Chinatown."

Once they were in the car and could talk freely, William asked, "Who owns the shop where the vortex is located?"

"We do," answered Frigga. "By we, I mean a holding company that has been buying up properties where vortexes are located. We want to protect the passages between our worlds because some of them have been destroyed. For example there used to be one in the Los Angeles area, but it is now covered by a freeway. A man who worked for us ran the shop in Chinatown, but we are afraid Hagen must have killed him. At any rate we had to find someone else to occupy the building."

Soon they were threading their way through the narrow, crowded streets of Chinatown. Parking was limited, and they had to leave the car nearly two blocks away from the shop. The children had never seen it from the front before, so as they walked, William asked, "Which one is it, Frigga?"

Frigga pointed down the street. "Do you see the sign with the red dragon?" she said. "That is it, The Red Dragon Locksmith Shop." The children, who were tired of sitting—first on the plane, then in the car—ran ahead and pushed open the door. The interior of the shop was decorated in Chinese fashion, but the man and the girl behind the counter were definitely not Chinese.

"Joe, Andrea! What are you doing here?" cried Susan.

"Ulysses asked us to take this place over," replied Joe. "This used to be a Chinese curio shop, but it was a perfect place for me to set up a locksmith business. Ulysses wants as few people as possible to know about the vortex, and we already did, so it was natural for him to ask us. He did not tell us how to make it work, however, because Andrea and I are not supposed to enter Earth-Two. We are only gate keepers."

That evening was a very pleasant one. The whole group had dinner in the apartment above the shop, where Andrea and her father now lived. Pete and Al had also been staying there for the past few days. They had sold all of their belongings because they were planning to stay in Earth-Two for the rest of their lives. Ulysses had said they could have the sailboat, and they planned to become fishermen or perhaps traders.

The next morning was Sunday, so they all went to church together. Al had been converted when he sailed with the children earlier that spring. Joe and Andrea became Christians shortly after they opened the locksmith shop, and Pete was still thinking about his relationship to God.

As they climbed back into the car after the service, Harold said, "The sermon was good, but I like our own Pastor Smith even better."

"So do I," said Susan, "and not just because of his sermons. Pastor Smith knows us and loves us. I think that makes a difference. This place is much larger than our little country church, but I suppose Joe and Andrea will feel close to their pastor after they get to know him better."

"I think he is very nice," said Andrea. "He always smiles at me, and he pays attention to me and the rest of the children. He doesn't just talk to the grownups. He acts just like Jesus did, as we learned last week in Sunday School. When the disciples tried to keep the children away from Jesus, He said, 'Permit the children to come to Me, and do not hinder them, for the kingdom of God belongs to such as these' (Luke 18:16). My teacher said that there are no little people in God's eyes."

"That is exactly right," said Frigga. There are no little people and no little jobs in God's kingdom. One time when King David was away from his family, enemies came and captured everyone and everything in his village. David and six hundred men chased after the enemies, but two hundred men were too tired to go all the way, so David left them to guard some of their stuff. He and the rest of his men rescued the women and children. They also recovered the sheep and cows and other things that the enemies had stolen.

"The four hundred men, who had gone all the way with David, did not want to share any of the spoils of battle with the two hundred tired soldiers. David, however, said, 'For as his share is who goes down to the battle, so shall his share be who stays by the baggage; they shall share alike' (1 Samuel 30:24). That is the way God deals with us. He will reward missionaries who go to other lands with the gospel, and He will also reward Christians who stay behind to give and pray for them. In the same way, Harold, Susan, and William are going to Earth-Two on a special mission, but God will reward you for staying behind and helping to watch over the vortex."

"Thank you, Frigga. I like that story," said Andrea thoughtfully. "I was wondering if I should volunteer to go with Susan and the boys, but I am so happy here with my father that I really do not want to be any place else. I'm glad this is God's place for me. It may look like a little place, but there are no little people and no little places in God's kingdom."

Early the next morning Pete and Al loaded some fresh fruit and vegetables and a few other supplies onto a two-wheeled cart in the basement of the shop. The children and Frigga strapped on their backpacks and all six of them departed from

Earth-One.

Pete and Al had already taken many loads down to the sailboat including canned food, clothing for themselves, a compass and other instruments for sailing, and some things Ulysses had suggested for trading. On this occasion they had to make two trips with the rowboat to ferry all the people and their baggage out to the sailboat. Then, since the tide had already begun to go out, they hoisted the sail and turned the boat toward the mouth of the Great Bay.

The trip north along the coast of northern California and Oregon was uneventful. Pete and Al were more experienced sailors now, and although they insisted on calling Harold "Captain," they were quite capable of managing everything by themselves. The weather was fair and the winds steady, so they were able to make very good progress. Still, it took them over a week to reach their destination.

Late one afternoon William was manning the tiller of the sailboat; Frigga was reading; Susan was napping, and Harold was leaning against the railing holding a fishing rod and staring absent-mindedly out to sea. "Catch anything, Captain?" Harold started at the sound, then relaxed as he turned and smiled.

"No, not yet, Al. You seem to have better luck at fishing than I do. Mostly I was just thinking about what lies ahead of us. We must be nearly to the mouth of the Columbia River by now."

"Yes, we are, Captain. That is what I came to tell you. The tide is flowing out, and by the time it turns we may not be able to sail up river and reach the village before dark. What do you want to do?"

"I'm anxious to get to the village, but I suppose it would be better to anchor off shore and to wait until after low tide tomorrow. What do you and the others think?"

"William wants to head up the river as soon as we can. Pete and I are for waiting until tomorrow. When Frigga heard us talking, she just glanced up from her book and asked, 'Why don't you ask the Captain?' So here I am."

Harold looked toward the back of the ship at Frigga. She had put her book down and was smiling at him. "Well, there isn't a cloud in the sky, and the barometer is holding steady. There is no reason to seek shelter, so tell William to bring us close enough to shore to drop anchor. We will make our grand entrance tomorrow."

Low tide arrived at seven the next morning, and shortly afterwards Captain Harold gave the order to weigh anchor and to head up the broad mouth of the Columbia River. Frigga joined William and Susan at the bow to watch for obstacles in the water while Harold and the men worked the sail and the tiller. Occasionally they had to make a quick change of course to avoid a sandbar or a partly submerged rock, but for the most part it was not difficult to stay in the channel. In some places the current of the river was stronger than the incoming tide, so progress was slow, but shortly before ten o'clock, William spotted the roofs of some houses. A few minutes later their boat rounded a bend in the river, and the whole village leaped into view.

Almost as quickly as they saw, they were seen. Even without binoculars the watchers in front could see a flurry of excited activity. Children jumped up and down and pointed across the water. Women let down their baskets to watch, and men set down their tools and fishing nets. In less than five minutes half a dozen canoes had put out from the shore.

"Are they going to be friendly, Frigga?" asked Susan. "What kind of welcome will they give us?"

"I wish I knew," replied the young woman. "All we can do now is wait."

CHAPTER 5—THE VILLAGE

When villagers had paddled to within fifty feet of the sailboat, a man in the lead canoe called out, "Cedric, Athelstane! Where are Cedric and Athelstane?"

Frigga stepped to the railing and stood tall so that her ranger cloak and medallion were clearly visible. "We know nothing of Cedric and Athelstane, but if they were once with this boat, they are no longer. It was found empty and anchored in the Great Bay. Do you have a pilot who can come on board and bring us to anchor at your village?"

"Aye, Ma'am, that would be my job," replied the same man. William threw the rope ladder over the side so that the man could climb up.

Harold, feeling bit awkward and uncertain, greeted him. "Welcome aboard, Master Pilot. I am Captain Harold Wilson. These are my crew and the ranger Miss Frigga. Will you please be so kind as to take the helm?"

The pilot stood for a moment with his mouth hanging open in surprise. Who had ever heard of a mere boy claiming to be a captain over two children and two grown men? Although he had never met a ranger before, he was certain they were supposed to be stern and strong. So why were the children dressed as rangers, except that their medallions were silver? And surely the most beautiful woman in the world could not be a ranger, could she?

Several seconds passed before the pilot finally managed to close his mouth. No one seemed to be laughing, so apparently this was no joke. He shook himself and replied, "John Little at your service, Sir."

Pilot Little expertly guided their craft around several large rocks to an anchorage near three sailboats similar to their own. In a short time the whole company was standing on the shore surrounded by a crowd of curious villagers.

The village consisted of ninety-seven dwellings of various sizes. (Out of curiosity William counted them one afternoon a few weeks into their visit.) All of them were made of stone with cedar shake shingles for roofs. The smallest houses consisted of three rooms: a bedroom for the parents, a bedroom for the children and a common room, which served as a kitchen and living room. Some of the larger houses were well planned with two stories built into a square around a central garden, but many of them looked like a jumble of smaller houses that had been stuck together in odd ways as their occupants increased in number.

The largest structure in the village was a three-story inn. The top floor was occupied by the innkeeper, his considerable family and his servants. The second story was for guests. The first floor housed the kitchen and an immense dining room, which served as the social hall for the village. It was to this building that the villagers led the little party of adventurers.

"Come. You must see the Grandmother," said John Little. "The president of our village council and several of the elders are away fishing or hunting or working on their farms. Besides they all listen to the Grandmother anyway."

The Grandmother was sitting in a rocking chair on the wide verandah of the inn. Several small children surrounded her, playing with rag dolls or tossing a ball in a game like jacks. William was drawn to her at once. He stared at her, which is most impolite, as Frigga and the old woman talked. She was old, much older than Ulysses, who had seen more than four hundred summers. William could never explain how he knew this. After all her skin was still smooth and when she stood, she held herself erect without stooping. But she was, without question, ancient. Centuries, both of hardship and of happiness, lay upon her. Her eyes were deep blue wells filled with wisdom and goodness.

William heard, as if in a dream, the formal introductions. He stepped forward and bowed his head, when his name was given, and then moved back into his place. He only half listened as Frigga talked. She had already drilled the children on the parts of their story they were allowed to share in the village. There was to be no mention of Ulysses or of Hagen and his band of rebels or of the voyage with the kidnapped children. Frigga told the Grandmother how the Harold, Susan, and William had accidentally entered Earth-Two through a vortex near their homes and said that she had been instructed to train them as potential rangers. When the sailboat was found abandoned at the Great Bay, she was assigned the task of returning it to the village where it had been made. She had brought the three children with her in hopes of leaving them at the village to learn about life in Earth-Two while she conducted a tour of villages to the north. Frigga concluded with a request that she be allowed to purchase the sailboat for her friends, Pete and Al, who planned to stay in Earth-Two.

The Grandmother listened attentively through Frigga's whole narration. Then for some time she said nothing, but sat humming and rocking in her chair. Finally she spoke. "I can see that your tale has been greatly shortened. There are many things you have not told me. Whether that is good or bad, I cannot say.

"No payment is necessary for the sailboat. A stranger named Hagen bought it several months ago. Your story suggests that the men who sailed it for him may no longer be alive. In that case, you may wish to make a charitable donation to their families. If you are willing to do that, I think no one will object to your friends using the boat until its owner calls for it."

"Thank you, Grandmother," replied Frigga.

"The innkeeper has rooms he can let out to Pete and Al," continued the Grandmother, "but I think it will be better if the children stay with one of the families. I feel certain there is a great deal more to them than you have said. We do not often see rangers in these parts, but many years ago I knew several rangers quite well. Children this young, who were chosen for training, would never have worn the cape and the silver medallion unless their talents and their accomplishments were extraordinary. For that reason, I will ask my grandson, whose house is next to mine, to keep the children. His son and daughter are about their age."

"You are indeed a wise woman, Grandmother," replied Frigga. "Again, I thank you."

The children stayed at the inn with Frigga that night. After washing up, they met Pete and Al and headed downstairs for supper. Every corner of the large hall was crammed full of people. All the villagers wanted to see the newcomers, and the servants were kept busy throughout the evening running back and forth from the kitchen with laden platters and full pitchers. When the little party of travelers appeared, the innkeeper cleared a table in the center of the room for their use, sending its former occupants to find places wherever they could.

"Everybody is watching us eat," said Susan. "I feel like an animal at the zoo." She was using mind-talk directed toward Harold and William.

Harold smiled and nodded. William flashed the two of them a mental picture of a monkey scratching under his armpit and eating a banana.

"How did you do that, William?" asked Susan.

"Yes, how did you send us a picture instead of words?" echoed Harold.

"I don't know. It just came out. Let me try again." This time

Susan and Harold saw a kangaroo hopping up and down on the back of an elephant.

Susan and William giggled. Harold started to laugh, but he choked on his supper and spent several seconds gasping for air. When he could breathe normally again, Frigga said sternly (aloud and in English), "I think I need to have a talk with the three of you when we go upstairs. Remember, we are guests here, so mind your manners."

The boys nodded and hung their heads; Susan blushed with shame. Pete and Al looked at each other and shrugged. They did not know about mind-talk, so they had no idea that anything unusual might be going on. After a few minutes the children began to relax again because one of the villagers stood up and began telling a story. Apparently, most of those present had heard it before because they started laughing before he reached the punch line. When he had finished, he pointed at their table and said, "Now it is your turn. One of you must tell us a story. Tell us what it is like to live in Earth-One."

The children looked questioningly at Frigga, who said (in English again), "Telling stories is one of their chief forms of amusement. Remember, they have no television and not many books, so when they get together they tell stories or sing songs. They hope we will tell them something they have not heard before. Does one of you want to take a turn?"

Susan and William looked at Harold. He was the oldest, and during the past year he had gradually become their leader. Harold glanced over at Frigga, who nodded and smiled approvingly. Reluctantly Harold stood up, but he was too short to see past the people immediately around their table. One of the villagers motioned toward the chair, so Harold stepped up on the seat, which was much better. He told them about electric lights and cars, but when a man asked what made cars run, he did not know how to answer, so he decided to skip computers and televisions. Instead he told them about their church and their school and about the bear Susan had called in to lick the face of the bully Lenny.[5] That brought a laugh, and Harold decided he could sit down.

Next the crowd tried to get a story from Pete or Al, but the men only knew a few sentences in the Mother Tongue. Al managed to say, "We do not understand your speech. We want to learn. We want to live here." Someone gave him a good-natured thump on the back, and the story telling passed on to other villagers. Although they were obviously interested in Frigga, no one dared to ask the beautiful ranger for a tale, and she did not offer one.

Sometime later, when the crowd began to sing, Frigga took the children up to bed. "Now for our little talk," she said, after she had shut the door. "Don't you realize how foolish it is to use mind-talk in such an open way? It was obvious to me that you were sharing secrets without opening your mouths, and if anyone near us was experienced in mind-talk it would have been clear to him as well."

"I'm sorry, Frigga. I guess I started it," said Susan.

Frigga gave her a quick hug and replied, "Well, maybe no harm was done, but you need to learn to be more discrete."

"That reminds me of a verse I read last week," said Harold. "Proverbs 11:22 says, 'As a ring of gold in a swine's snout So is a beautiful woman who lacks discretion.'"

Both boys started giggling until Frigga said sharply, ""Harold, William. I think we could say the same thing about two handsome boys who lack discretion. Your good looks are no better than a gold ring in the nose of a pig if you can't learn to think before you speak."

Harold and William apologized to Susan. It was a sincere

---

[5] See the last chapter of *The Vortex*.

apology because the three children really did love each other.

Then Frigga spoke again. "I want to ask one more thing before you go to bed. Have you learned to hold a three-way conversation in mind-talk? I have had suspicions for some time, and tonight all three of you laughed at the same moment. So tell me what is going on."

"Yes, we have," replied Susan. "We were wondering how long it would take you to catch on."

Eagerly the three children described how they had learned to share in the same mind-talk conversation. "As for tonight," concluded Harold, "Susan said she felt like an animal at the zoo, and when William sent us a couple of funny pictures, we simply could not help laughing."

"You sent them what?" demanded Frigga, looking at William.

Instead of answering aloud, William sent Frigga the same mental images he had given to Harold and Susan at the dinner table. Frigga was so amazed she virtually fell into a chair and sat there for a few moments with her mouth open. Finally she said, "Ulysses told me no one had ever succeeded in linking three minds, and I am almost positive that sending mental pictures is exceedingly rare too. Susan and Harold, can do that?"

They could not, either that night or afterwards. The next time Frigga reported by mind-talk to Ulysses, she described William's unique ability, and he was nearly as surprised as she.

CHAPTER 6—THE GRANDMOTHER

Two days after they arrived, Frigga bought a horse and took the local ferry across the great river to begin her inspection of villages to the north. After she left, the children moved into their new quarters next door to the house of the Grandmother. She actually was the grandmother several times removed for about half of the village, and everyone else called her that. Likewise, she called all of her descendants her grandchildren, no matter how many generations lay between them.

As the Grandmother led them toward their new lodgings, she said, "I would like for you to come and talk to me for a while each day that you are in the village."

"That would be nice," answered Susan, but in her mind she heard William asking, "Was that an invitation or an order?"

"Same thing in this case," was Harold's reply. "The Grandmother may be gentle and kind, but whatever she says goes. Haven't you noticed she never says anything twice?"

Susan started to nod, and then caught herself. "Be careful, you two. I almost nodded my head. I am sure she would have noticed. She doesn't miss a trick!"

The children's mind-talk was cut short because the Grandmother was speaking again. "This is the house where you will be staying. I live over there. Your hosts are Locksley and his wife Anne. Their children are Robin and Marian." The Grandmother knocked on the door and entered without waiting for a response.

After introductions and a few minutes of polite conversation, the Grandmother handed Locksley a small bag of gold that Frigga had left to pay for the children's room and board. Then she dismissed them saying, "Robin and Marian, please show

Harold, Susan, and William their rooms. Then you may all go out to play. I think it will be all right for you to take some bread and cheese with you for lunch. Come back in time for supper. I want to spend a while with your parents in private."

The house, which had once been occupied by a larger family, turned out to be a regular labyrinth. William called it the Higgledy-Piggledy house because the various sections of the house were oddly shaped and joined together at funny angles. "It would be easy to get lost in here," remarked Susan as the children threaded their way single file through an especially narrow corridor.

"Don't worry," laughed Marian. "You will get used to it. This is the best house in the village for playing hide and seek on a rainy day. Here are your rooms. We call this section the round rooms. The outer wall is a circle except here at the door where it joins the rest of the house. Your bedrooms are on the outside of the circle and in the middle is a round living room."

The children from Earth-One deposited their knapsacks in their rooms and then followed Robin and Marian outside. Several other children were waiting for them, and soon the whole group was headed out of the village. Robin was the biggest of the boys and the natural leader of the group. The older children, both boys and girls were all busy. Their formal schooling stopped when they were thirteen years old, and they began to learn a trade. Therefore the younger children were on their summer break, but the older ones were hard at work.

Throughout the afternoon, the village children led Harold, Susan, and William to see all of their favorite haunts—the best swimming hole (which was still too cold to use), the deep gully that was bridged by only two ropes (one for the feet and the other for the hands), and the climbing cliff (which was responsible for more than one broken bone). The children arrived back home at exactly the right time for supper. Even though there were no watches in Earth-Two, everyone knew how to tell time by the position of the sun.

Over the next few days, life settled down into a fairly regular routine. Harold, Susan, and William spent the hour before breakfast having devotions from the Bible Susan had brought and reviewing the vocabulary and skills Frigga had taught them. They also spent some time unpacking the information Ulysses had put into their heads during their super speed mind-talk session.

After breakfast they helped out with chores around the house. There were always floors to sweep, wood to chop, and water to haul for washing dishes and clothes. In the afternoon they were free to do as they pleased. Sometimes that meant playing with the other children, but Harold also enjoyed working with Locksley at his blacksmith shop. Susan was fascinated with Anne's loom, so the woman began teaching her how to weave cloth. Every evening after supper the three Earth-One children went by themselves to visit the Grandmother.

Those times were always very interesting. They talked about life in Earth-One, and the Grandmother told them stories of her youth. She spoke fondly of her dead husband and their decision to move to this coast. They were the first settlers to come to the region. "Life was much harder then," she said one evening. "We had no houses, no wagons, no boats and very few tools. We knew how to fashion those things, but it took us many years to make life relatively comfortable. One thing we did not expect was that our children would become too busy at building a city in the wilderness. Hard work seemed to take up all of their time and energy. They had no desire to learn the history of our people or the harder lessons of the Mother Tongue. I have so much to teach, but no one who wants to learn. Many of them have even turned away from God. The meeting hall at the inn should be overflowing with worshipers on Sunday morning, but it is usually only half full. My children have become proud of their accomplishments and have forgotten that God is the one who gives them strength to labor."

The Grandmother stopped speaking, and the children watched her in silence. The long centuries of her life seemed to be pressing upon her, weighing her down with cares and grief. The mood lasted only a few moments. Then the Grandmother shook her head as if dismissing those dismal thoughts and sang the children a silly song she had learned as a girl.

The woodpecker pecked out a little round hole
In the trunk of an old oak tree.
Then he stuck in his head through that little round hole
For to see what he could see.

It was hollow inside like a very large cave
In the trunk of that old oak tree,
And the silly wee bird thought that he had made
All the space that he could see.

"What a job I've done to make all this room
In the trunk of the old oak tree,"
Said the proud little bird, as though someone heard
And his work might come to see.

The woodpecker's head soon began to swell
In the trunk of the old oak tree,
And his pride made it grow too large for the hole,
So he could not pull it free.

So his tail's in the air, and his head's in the hole
Of the trunk of that old oak tree,
And I think there's a lesson or maybe two
For the likes of you and me.

The children laughed, and William flashed them a mental picture of the woodpecker with a greatly enlarged head stuck in the hole of a tree, which provoked fresh bursts of laughter. The Grandmother looked at them sharply, and said, "You know what the lesson is, I suppose."

"Yes Grandmother," replied William. "It is the lesson of Proverbs 16:18 'Pride goes before destruction, And a haughty spirit before stumbling.'"

"Very good, William. Frigga has taught you well, but you are not yet careful enough. I believe she has left you here for more reasons than one. I do not know what she has in mind, but if you let your training and the trust she has placed in you go to your head, you may fail. Worse than that, you may find yourself in as much trouble as the silly woodpecker."

Later that evening back in their own quarters, Susan said, "I have the feeling that every time we talk to the Grandmother she learns more about us than we have actually told her. I saw her eyes flicker with interest the other day when we recognized the name of one of the great rangers from long ago. Then tonight I am sure she knew that some hidden joke passed between us at the end of her song. Either we must be more careful, or we should tell her everything. What do you think, Harold?"

Harold sat quietly for a minute or two, then said, "I will try to contact Ulysses before I go to sleep tonight. He is far away, and mind-talk will be difficult, but we need his advice."

Susan and William nodded, and the three children readied themselves for bed. Harold lay awake for some time waiting for the rest of the household to fall asleep. He did not want any interruptions from their hosts while he was trying to concentrate. In the stillness of the night he tried to reach out with his mind to Ulysses. At his first attempt he got no reply.

His second attempt was also a failure, but on his third try Ulysses answered. Quickly Harold explained their concerns.

"You are right, Harold, to be perplexed. I know of the Grandmother. She is a woman of great knowledge and strength. She will be either your greatest ally, or your most dangerous enemy. I do not know which. I am afraid you will have to be guided by your own sense of what is best. For now I think that caution is in order, but the three of you will have to choose your own course. I have been praying that God will guide you; you should do the same." Harold fell asleep doing just that.

Although the children continued to enjoy their visits with the Grandmother, Ulysses' warning troubled their hearts. Perhaps the Grandmother noticed. At any rate she asked them very few questions and seemed content to talk about whatever subject they chose. One evening about a week after Ulysses' warning, something occurred that affected the whole future course of their adventure.

The children were sitting with the Grandmother on her verandah when four men arrived carrying a young boy on a stretcher. The lad had fallen from a tree house and broken his leg below the knee. One of the bones had pierced the skin, and the boy was wailing loudly. The Grandmother stepped quickly to his side, touched his head and leaned over to whisper in his ear. Instantly the boy fell asleep.

"Lay him down on my bed," she commanded. With the help of the boy's uncle, she pulled the bone back into place. Then she knelt beside the bed and wrapped her hands around the injury. For perhaps twenty minutes she remained motionless beside the boy, except for the silent moving of her lips. Then she stood up. The hole where the bone had broken through the skin was gone.

"The boy will be sore for a few days," she said. "He may stand and walk a little in the house, but do not allow him to go outside to play for at least three weeks."

After the men had taken the boy away, the Grandmother sank into a chair and said to the children, "You had better go now. I am very tired." Harold and Susan left immediately, but William did not move.

"Grandmother," he said. "I can heal too, at least a little bit. I could have put the boy to sleep, but I do not know how to care for a broken leg. Will you teach me?"

The Grandmother looked at him fondly and smiled. "So you have decided to trust me with at least one of your secrets. Yes, William. I will teach you."

CHAPTER 7—LESSONS AND SUSPICIONS

William's training began the next day. He left for the Grandmother's house every morning immediately after breakfast and did not return until suppertime.

"The Grandmother makes Frigga's training look like a picnic," he said one evening. "She is making me learn all the parts of the body—every organ, every bone, every major blood vessel, and what each part does. I think I have seen the insides of every chicken or duck butchered in the village in the past week. Tomorrow she is taking me out to one of the farms where they are slaughtering a sheep and a pig. They are much more like human beings than fish or birds are."

"But why do you need to know all that stuff?" asked Susan.

"The Grandmother says that the healing she does is not like the miraculous healings in the Bible. When God healed people with a miracle, the prophet or apostle did not need to know anything about what was going on in the sick person's body. She is more like a surgeon. A surgeon uses a knife to cut, and he uses sutures to sew things back together. She uses her mind to cut or to sew or to kill a cancer, so she needs to know where everything is and how it works."

"A good healer needs to be able to see things in his mind. I can do that. When I place my hand on your arm like this, Susan, and say the proper word in the Mother Tongue for one of your bones, I can see that bone in my mind. If your bone is broken, I can see in my mind how your bone differs from the look of a perfect bone. Healing means putting each part back the way it should be. The Grandmother is very good at this. She can put small blood vessels and torn muscles back together, but she says it will be a long time before I can do that."

"I think God must have brought us here so that you could be trained by her," said Susan thoughtfully.

"That is what the Grandmother said too," replied William. "She says it has been a very long time since she had someone to teach, someone who was both able and willing to learn."

"Well, it is nice to see some good thing coming out of this visit," said Harold. "We do not seem to have made any progress on solving Ulysses' mysteries. I hope he is not disappointed. No one here knows why Hagen wanted to buy a boat, and no one knows why he came here to purchase it instead of stopping somewhere closer to the Great Bay. I am having a great time and learning quite a bit about Earth-Two, but I have not seen one suspicious-looking person since we came here."

"I have," said William.

"What? What didn't you tell us?" asked Harold.

"I have been so busy it never occurred to me that he was out of the ordinary until you said we have not seen anyone who looked suspicious. Have you noticed the tall man who always wears a leather hat with a feather in it?"

"Yes," replied Susan, "but what is unusual about him?"

"Two things," answered William. "First, he does not seem to have a job. He just hangs around the village as though he had nothing else to do. Second, I think he is watching the Grandmother. I must see him eight or ten times a day—just strolling by her house or leaning against a tree. Yesterday when the Grandmother and I went up river to take care of a sick child, he came hiking by the house twirling his walking stick and humming a tune. I was sitting on the porch drinking apple juice. He looked straight at me and then turned away without saying a word. I don't know anything about him, but maybe we should ask around."

Harold and Susan agreed, and by the next evening they were all sure that William's suspicions had been right on target. The man's name was Loki. He was not a native of the village but had arrived two days after Hagen. Even though no one had actually seen them talking together, they both stayed at the inn, so they might have been plotting at night. Loki seemed to have plenty of money; he paid for whatever he wanted in gold and silver. Other than these few facts no one seemed to know him very well.

All of this information had been learned by Harold and Susan, but the most disturbing news came from William. "I am sure the Grandmother knows more than she is willing to tell," he said. "I tried three times to ask her about Loki. The first time she just said, 'He is a stranger to our village,' and then she started quizzing me about muscles and tendons in the leg. The second time she ignored my question. The third time she actually snapped at me. She said, 'Be still, William, or I will send you back home tomorrow to pester your mother with your foolish questions.' The Grandmother does not make empty threats, so I shut up."

Later that night Harold reported their suspicions to Ulysses using mind-talk. "Go wake up William," said Ulysses. "I want to know exactly what the man looks like."

So Harold woke both William and Susan. William sat up and rubbed his eyes. Almost immediately the voice of Ulysses spoke in his head: "Can you send me a mind picture of Loki?"

William concentrated. It was very difficult to send something as complex as a picture over a long distance, but after a few minutes he succeeded. For a moment Ulysses said nothing. Then in rapid succession he sent the same message to each of the children: "Be very careful. That is the most dangerous man in two worlds. I will be there as soon as I can, and I will summon Frigga back to the village as well."

For several minutes the children sat together in stunned silence. Finally Susan spoke. "Ulysses is afraid. I could hear it in his voice." Harold and William nodded.

"I am afraid, too," said William.

"We all are" replied Harold. "Susan, can you think of a Bible verse about fear? I know that I should be able to come up with something, but right now my mind is a blank."

Susan went to her room and returned with her Bible. Slowly she turned the pages until she found the place. Then by the light of a flickering candle she read, "Do not fear, for I am with you; Do not anxiously look about you, for I am your God. I will strengthen you, surely I will help you, Surely I will uphold you with My righteous right hand" (Isaiah 41:10). She repeated the words several times. After that the three children held hands, bowed their heads and prayed. Then they went to their beds with God's promise echoing in their hearts.

Susan and Harold spent the next day wandering aimlessly about the house or sitting on the porch and staring down at the river. Anne noticed their moodiness, and so did the Grandmother. "What is wrong, children?" she asked during their evening visit. "William has been nervous and unable to concentrate all day long. Now you two look as glum as a couple of mules."

Susan and William glanced over at Harold, who shrugged and answered for all of them. "I guess we just had a bad day. Maybe we will all feel better tomorrow."

The Grandmother looked sharply at them. "I hope so. If not, you will have to come up with a better answer next time I ask." Then she sent them home and told them to go to bed early.

The next morning at breakfast Anne announced that the children were free of chores for the day and could do whatever they wanted. William chose to go to the Grandmother's as usual; Harold and Robin took a canoe to paddle up river looking for turtles; Susan and Marian decided to hike to an abandoned tourmaline mine located in the hills about an hour away. The mine was mostly worked out, but Marian had once found a small but beautiful pink crystal there, and Susan hoped to do the same.

William knocked at the Grandmother's door and entered without waiting for an answer. She was seated by the window, working at her loom. "I thought you had the day off to play, William. Why have you come?"

"If it is no trouble, Grandmother, I would like to continue my lessons. I have this one summer with you, and who knows if I will ever be able to come back? May I go to see Pete and Al for a few minutes before we begin? I saw their sailboat at anchor, so they must have come back from their fishing trip late last night."

"Certainly, William," she replied. "I will be here when you return."

William was only gone for about thirty minutes, but in that time he quickly briefed Pete and Al on what they had learned about Loki. Then he added, "I will feel better if you two stay in the village until either Frigga or Ulysses arrives."

The men were happy to agree. "Don't worry, William" said Al. "We will take turns keeping an eye on this Loki fellow for you. That way it won't be as obvious as if both of us were watching him all the time."

William went back to the Grandmother's with a happier heart. It helped to be able to tell his problems to two grownups, and it never occurred to him to ask how his friends might be able to deal with the most dangerous man in two worlds. Every once in a while throughout the morning William saw either Pete or Al moving about the village, and their presence helped him to relax and work.

Shortly before noon, the Grandmother was weaving at her loom as she supervised William's studies. He was carefully cutting apart the heart of a pig, learning the names of each valve and chamber and blood vessel. Then using the Mother Tongue and his own special gift he compared what he saw with what he could sense and imagine in his own beating heart. Suddenly he dropped his tools and looked up at the Grandmother. His face was pale, and his hands were shaking. "I can't reach Susan's mind," he said. "Neither can Harold. That means she is either unconscious or dead."

CHAPTER 8—THE RESCUE

So you can use mind-talk," said the Grandmother. "I am not surprised." She left her loom and knelt beside William to put her arms around his shaking body. "Now tell me what you know. Where is Harold? Where was Susan when you last had contact with her?"

"Harold is up the river in a canoe with Robin. Right now they are at Council Rock. Susan and Marian went to the old tourmaline mine to look for crystals. Harold thinks the roof must have caved in because when he talked to her a few minutes ago they were farther back in the mine than Marian had ever been before."

The Grandmother took William by his shoulders, held him at arms' length and looked him square in the eye as she spoke. "William, you must calm down. Your sister's life may depend on it. Remember that God is King over all the earth. He holds your life and the life of your sister in His hands. If she has perished, the Lord Jesus will give you strength to bear it. If she lives, He may give us strength to rescue her. And Marian. Don't forget Marian. Now this is what I want you to do. Contact Harold. Tell him and Robin to cut across country to the mine. On the way they will pass a couple of farms where they should be able to recruit help. They are not far from the mine and may be able to reach it before we can. After you have talked to Harold, go to the stable and fetch my horse. You can ride behind me. Meanwhile I will have my grandson next door call the men of the village together."

Ten minutes later the Grandmother and William were cantering along the trail that led to the old mine. On horseback it would only take them about thirty minutes. Most of the villagers would take longer since they needed to gather tools and since many of them did not have horses. The Grandmother and William rounded the last curve in the trail just in time to see Harold emerging from the old mineshaft. His cheeks were covered with dust through which little rivers of tears had recently flown, but when he spoke, his voice was firm.

"Grandmother, there has been a cave-in, just as I suspected, but the men do not want to start removing the rubble until they have some wood to shore up the roof of the tunnel. They are afraid more rocks will fall as soon as these are taken away. I told them that I could support the roof with an air shield, but I don't think they believe me because they have ever heard of such a thing. Will you speak to them?"

"Yes, Harold," she replied. "Air shields of various kinds have long been used by the rangers, but not many outside their circles know how to make them. The people in these parts have had little contact with rangers, but they will listen to me."

From a sack tied to her saddle the Grandmother pulled out a stick. One end of the stick was covered with pitch, and when she spoke in the Mother Tongue, the pitch burst into flame. Holding her torch up over her head, she stepped quickly into the tunnel with the two boys following close behind.

The first twenty yards of the tunnel had a wooden ceiling, which was supported every few feet by massive wooden posts. After that there was only solid rock overhead, but wherever the tunnel widened out into a larger room, the miners had left columns of stone to support the roof. The little group passed three such rooms before they reached the cave-in. Four very nervous farmers were standing a few feet away from a heap of rocks that reached from the floor to the ceiling. They were talking in whispers because they feared that any loud noise might cause a further collapse of the stone overhead.

As soon as the Grandmother arrived, she took charge. Under

her direction Harold and William made an air shield to protect the workers from falling rocks. Then Grandmother told the farmers what to do. Her orders mostly sounded like this: "Next remove that large round stone and place it over here. The jagged piece goes over there." So skillful were her instructions that the tunnel through the rubble would probably have held up even without the help of Harold and William.

Harold watched with growing surprise at the progress and said in mind-talk to William, "Is there anything the Grandmother cannot do?"

"Yes," answered William. "Even she cannot bring the dead to life."

After what seemed like a long time, men from the village arrived with tools and with wood to make a protective ceiling. Still working under the Grandmother's direction, the men quickly shored up the sides and roof of the tunnel through the rubble. After that the danger of a cave-in was much less, so Harold and William took turns maintaining a smaller air shield for the man working at the front of the tunnel. Sometime later, one of the workmen called for quiet. When all was still, a gentle tapping of stone on stone came from the far side of the cave-in.

"Well, I'm glad that at least Marian is alive," said William.

"How do you know it is Marian, and not Susan?" asked a farmer who had come with Harold. "Now that I think of it, how did Harold know the girls were trapped?"

"Enough talk," interrupted the Grandmother. "Back to work, everyone."

As the men settled into their tasks, a slight movement at the edge of William's vision caused him to turn around. The shadow of a man retreating back up the tunnel flickered briefly on the wall, then disappeared. William could not be sure, but he thought he recognized the profile of Loki.

Although it felt like days, it really only took about three

hours for the men to make a passage through the rubble. As soon as the breakthrough was announced, the Grandmother touched William on the shoulder and said, "Follow me. The rest of you wait here until we are through. Then build a roof to support the last few feet."

Two thirds of the way through the tunnel, William and the Grandmother squeezed past Harold who was maintaining the air shield. The passage at the far end was quite narrow, so William, who was behind the Grandmother, heard Marian before he saw her. "Oh, Grandmother! Oh, Grandmother! Oh, Grandmother!" That was all she could say between her sobs.

A moment later William crawled through the opening to see the bloodstained face and head of his sister cradled in the lap of her friend. He reached her side only seconds after the Grandmother and gently touched her neck with his hand. Whispering quietly in the Mother Tongue he began to probe her body with his mind, and with his mind he spoke to his best friend.

"Susan is alive, Harold. Her heart is strong and her breathing regular. There is a gash on her head, and she is unconscious. I don't know how serious it is. The Grandmother is working on her head injury already. There is nothing I can do to help, but if I place my hands beside hers, I may be able to watch what is going on inside Susan's skull."

So Harold waited and William watched. With the wonderful picture-making ability of his mind he saw the place where Susan's brain had been injured by falling rock. He saw that the bleeding in the brain had stopped and that her body had already begun to heal itself, and he saw how the Grandmother hastened and helped the healing process.

Susan woke up to find her brother and her best friend kneeling by her side. "I'm glad you are back," said Harold. "I was afraid you were dead, and I didn't know what I would do if you were, and I. . . ." Harold's heart was full, but he had run out of words. He leaned over and gently brushed Susan's cheek with the back of one finger. "How do you feel?" he asked.

Susan smiled weakly and answered, "My head hurts."

"It will continue to hurt for a day or two," said the Grandmother, who was standing near the tunnel. "God be praised, the injury was not a serious one, but I don't want you to move any more than is necessary until tomorrow, and even then you must take it easy. Soon the tunnel will be wide enough for the men to pull you through on a stretcher."

Back at the village that evening, Locksley stood on the porch in front of his house before a large group of his Christian neighbors, and together they praised God. Over and over the neighbors chanted the first verse of Psalm 107. After each repetition Locksley loudly proclaimed one thing for which he was thankful.

Oh give thanks to the LORD, for He is good,
For His lovingkindness is everlasting.
The Lord has delivered my daughter.

Oh give thanks to the LORD, for He is good,
For His lovingkindness is everlasting.
The Lord has delivered my Marian.

Oh give thanks to the LORD, for He is good,
For His lovingkindness is everlasting.
The Lord has delivered my daughter's friend.

Oh give thanks to the LORD, for He is good,
For His lovingkindness is everlasting.
The Lord has delivered dear Susan.

Oh give thanks to the LORD, for He is good,

For His lovingkindness is everlasting.
The Lord warned Harold and William.

Oh give thanks to the LORD, for He is good,
For His lovingkindness is everlasting.
The Lord sent the ancient Grandmother.

Oh give thanks to the LORD, for He is good,
For His lovingkindness is everlasting.
The Lord sent the Grandmother to heal.

The chanting went on for quite some time as Locksley rehearsed all the details of the rescue a line at a time. The children were permitted to listen and watch for a few minutes. Then Anne fed them supper and sent them to bed.

Later that night, as the village slept, the Grandmother lay on her bed and reached out halfway around the world to the mind of her son. "What have you done?" she demanded. "Did you think you could protect me by sending three children? How do you expect them to face up to him?"

"I did not send them, Mother. Ulysses does not know whom to trust right now, and I don't blame him. Perhaps he sent them, but if so, he didn't consult with me when he came up with his plan."

At the same moment two other minds were also linked halfway around the globe, and Hagen was saying to Loki, "Kill the old woman and those three brats tomorrow. Then get out of town before Ulysses and that turncoat Frigga show up."

CHAPTER 9—HAROLD DISOBEYS

Shortly after midnight, the Grandmother slipped quietly into the round rooms of Locksley's home. Silently she shut the door behind her. Then she lit a small oil lamp and knocked softly, first on Harold's door and then on William's. A few seconds later the two boys stumbled out sleepily into the circular living room where the Grandmother was waiting.

She spoke in a whisper, but there was a note of urgency in her voice. "Most of the villagers have never even heard of air shields or mind-talk before. After today's rescue at the mine, however, everyone knows that you children have special abilities. I fear that you are in great danger."

"From Loki?" asked William.

The Grandmother hesitated before answering. "Yes, from Loki," she said. "I want you to contact Frigga and ask her to return as quickly as possible. And if you know of any other rangers in these parts, alert them as well."

"Frigga is already on her way, and so is Ulysses," answered Harold.

"Ulysses, the Wanderer! Or Odysseus, as we used to call him—God be praised! In days to come songs will be sung about the deeds of that man. How soon will it be before they arrive?" The Grandmother's voice and face brightened as she spoke.

"I do not know," replied Harold. "They hoped to be back by tomorrow, but Frigga's horse has come up lame. Ulysses is sailing toward us from the south, but the winds have turned against him. It could be two or three days before either of them makes it."

"Two or three days! So long?" The Grandmother sighed. "Well, we do what we must with the lot the Lord gives us." The

Grandmother sat quietly for a few moments, and then turned to the younger boy. "William," she said, "I want you to link minds with me. It is possible that I will not be able to continue your training in healing, so I want to give you as much knowledge as I can tonight."

William looked puzzled and distressed, but for once in his life he asked no questions. He simply nodded and said, "Before we came here Ulysses taught us in super speed using mind-talk, so if that is what you plan to do, I already understand the process."

William and the Grandmother began the mind-talk chant together, and in a surprisingly short time their minds were linked. Then the Grandmother placed her hands on the boy's head and began filling his mind with information about all the parts of the human body—what they look like, what they do, and how various diseases and injuries might be treated. When she was done, she removed her hands and William slumped over in his chair. He might have fallen to the floor except that Harold caught and steadied him. Then Harold and the Grandmother helped him back to bed.

When they were done, Harold and the Grandmother went back into the living room. The ancient lady placed her hands on the boy's shoulders and said, "Harold, please contact Ulysses and Frigga again. Tell them to come with all speed for danger is upon us. I want you and the other children to stay here in the house all day tomorrow and afterward until either Frigga or Ulysses comes. Susan and William should rest most of the day anyway. Do not tell Locksley, Anne or the other villagers your fears about Loki. If they tried to capture him, many of them might be killed."

Harold nodded; then as the Grandmother turned to leave, he said, "May I pray for you, and will you please pray with me?"

"Gladly, Harold."

For half an hour the two held hands as they turned their hearts toward their Heavenly Father. Finally they said, "Amen" together.

"I needed that, Harold. Thank you. Many people ask me to pray for them, but few actually pray with me. They think that I am strong and wise and so have no needs of my own. Perhaps they have forgotten that even the Apostle Paul said, "Brethren, pray for us" (1 Thessalonians 5:25). Even the strongest follower of Jesus may be strengthened by the weakest.

"Please tell William not to try to contact me with mind-talk tomorrow. I will not be answering him. Goodbye, Harold." With that she stepped to the door and in a moment was gone.

After the door had shut behind her, Harold stood still in the middle of the room for several minutes. Something was very wrong; something dreadful was about to happen. The Grandmother's "Goodbye" had sounded so final, as if she did not expect to see him again. But why? What did she know or guess? What did she plan to do?

Harold went to his bed, but before he used Frigga's special trick to put himself to sleep, he reported his conversation with the Grandmother to Ulysses and then to Frigga. He woke the next morning still troubled and went to breakfast alone because William and Susan were still sleeping. After breakfast he headed for the door to look up Pete and Al, but Anne stopped him with a hand on his shoulder and a stern voice. "Harold, the Grandmother said you were not to go out of the house today at all."

"I want to talk to our friends from Earth-One, Anne. If I cannot go out, will you allow Robin or Marian to find them for me?"

Anne agreed and a short time later Harold was conducting the two men back to the round rooms. Quickly he briefed them on what had happened during the night. "I believe," he said, "that Loki may make his move today. I know the Grandmother gave orders for us to stay in the house, but Ulysses sent us here to help. When I reported to him last night, he did not insist that we stay indoors. All he said was, 'Be careful.' If you can you find a ladder, I would like you to hide it in the bushes near the back bedroom window of the round rooms. Then if either Loki or the Grandmother does anything out of the ordinary, come in that way to tell us. Will you do that for me?"

"Sure, Harold " answered, Pete.

"Aye, aye, Captain," echoed Al, with a grin. "Life around you is never dull, is it?"

The men did not return that morning or throughout the afternoon. Susan and William spent most of the day sleeping, except that William got up for three snacks in addition to a late breakfast and lunch. Harold was bored because Locksley had sent his children to spend a couple of days with cousins who lived on a farm. Although no explanation was given, Harold was sure that the Grandmother wanted Robin and Marian out of harm's way. Supper was a pretty glum affair; everyone was tense. Locksley and Anne did not seem to want to talk.

Harold, whose fear of approaching disaster had been mounting all day, insisted that Susan and William come directly back to their rooms after the meal. They were sitting together in their little round living room talking softly and playing an Earth-Two game called sticks and stones when Pete climbed through the bedroom window and stepped into the living room.

"Spy number two reporting, Captain," he said, with just the smallest flicker of a grin. "Spy number one is hiding the ladder in the bushes until I signal him."

Harold rose to his feet. His palms were suddenly sweaty, and his voice quavered just a little as he asked, "What happened, Pete?"

"The Grandmother decided to take a walk in the woods. That is all. I said it was not important enough to report, but Al insisted we come. There was no one around, not even that stinker Loki. She had been sitting on her porch for an hour or so when she suddenly stood and headed up the path that leads from behind her house into the woods."

Harold sank down into his chair, put his hands to his cheeks and stared at the floor. "This is wrong. It is all wrong. What is she doing?"

Suddenly he leaped to his feet. "Loki was there even if you did not see him. I'm sure of it. He has been watching the Grandmother like an owl ready to swoop down on a baby rabbit. The Grandmother has gone into the woods to lure him there. She intends to face him by herself somewhere away from the village because she does not want anyone else to be hurt. That is the reason she wanted us to stay inside. That is the reason she insisted on teaching William last night; she was afraid she might not come back. Susan! William! I'm going after her. Do you feel well enough to come?"

Both children nodded and within three minutes they and the two men were following Harold up the path into the woods. Harold trotted rather than ran, but he kept a steady pace. Susan and William were able to keep up with him, but Pete and Al soon lagged behind. The children had been careful to maintain the exercise routine Frigga had given them, and now it paid off.

About twenty minutes up the trail the children came to the crest of a little hill overlooking a meadow. Ordinarily the music of the stream bubbling through a patchwork quilt of wildflowers would have been pure delight, but now the long shadows of evening fell across a scene that made their hearts stop.

The Grandmother stood quietly beside the stream in the midst of the meadow with her back toward them. Loki was stalking her, moving stealthily up the path behind her. He looked like a cat ready to pounce on a mouse. "Grandmother," screamed William with his mind. But there was no answer.

"Why won't she answer? Why is she just standing there? She must know that Loki is behind her. Why doesn't she turn and face him?" William's voice was almost weeping in the minds of Harold and Susan.

"I was wrong," answered Harold. "She did not come here to fight Loki. She came here to die. She came here to sacrifice herself for us."

As Harold's mind spoke these words, Loki leaned back and hurled a huge stone at the Grandmother. It was well aimed, or perhaps guided by words of the Mother Tongue, because it struck her solidly in the back of the head. Even as she crumpled to the ground William screamed the horrible words he had first heard from Hagen a few months ago. Loki grabbed his head and staggered. William screamed again, and Loki went down.

"Run, Harold! Run, Susan! He is very strong, so he will only be out for a few seconds."

The three children raced through the meadow to the still form of the Grandmother. Immediately William knelt beside her and placed his hands on her head. As William had predicted, Loki was back up on his feet almost before Harold and Susan had turned around to face him. He raised one arm and pointed an evil finger at the children, but before he could speak Harold grabbed Susan's hand and the two of them erected an air shield over themselves and over William and the Grandmother.

Now you must know that air shields are of different kinds. Some are hard; others are soft. Some work well against one kind of threat but not against others. One of the chief things Ulysses had taught them during his super-speed mind-talk session was how to alter an air shield to meet any kind of attack. Harold found that he needed everything they had learned. With Susan following his lead and lending her strength to him, he met stones and bolts of lightning and blasts of hot air and a wall of flame.

Loki was obviously frustrated and angry at finding such abilities in mere children, but he was strong and they were growing weaker. Susan, who had not fully recovered from her head injury, wobbled on her feet and then sank to her knees. As she did, she saw Pete and Al jump at Loki from behind. For a moment Loki turned his attention from the children to the men. He tossed them away from him like a bull tossing an unlucky matador with his horns. Pete and Al lay still in the meadow, one on either side of Loki. The assassin turned, fixed his gaze on Harold and shouted with a mighty voice. Suddenly a wall of dirt and stones rose up from the ground to rain down upon the weary children. Susan surrendered her last bit of strength to Harold, and the air shield held, but darkness closed in around her, and she knew no more.

CHAPTER 10—THE END

Susan awoke several hours after the rooster had greeted the rising sun. She rolled over onto her back, stretched out her arms and legs and wiggled her toes. Then she opened her eyes. "Why is it so light outside?" she wondered. "Why didn't Anne wake me up?" Then like a thunderbolt from a clear blue sky it came to her. "Loki!" she screamed.

She sat up, clutching her blanket, and a movement in the corner of the room caught her eye. Gold flashed on a color-shifting ranger cloak as Frigga stepped out of the shadows and sat down on the edge of her bed. "Do not be afraid, Susan. It is only I."

"O Frigga, thank God you are here. When did you come? Where is Loki? Are Harold, William and the Grandmother all right? And how about Pete and Al?"

"Yes, dear, they are all fine. I found a fresh horse to replace my lame one yesterday morning. God also answered our prayers and turned the wind around so that Ulysses and PC were able to reach the anchorage here just as the ferryman brought my horse and me across the river. One of the children had seen you running up the path, so we followed. When we reached the meadow, Harold was still standing. Somehow he had managed to hold off Loki for several minutes after you collapsed. Ulysses and I would like to have captured the traitor alive for questioning, but that was not possible. He is dead. Fortunately William was able to stop the bleeding in the Grandmother's brain before there was any damage. They both woke up an hour or so ago. If you get up and get dressed quickly, you can join everybody for lunch."

Ten minutes later Susan took her place at the table between

Harold and William. Pete, Al and the Grandmother sat opposite them with Ulysses and Frigga at either end. Lunch turned out to be a feast. Anne had been cooking since early in the morning, and she kept her husband busy going back and forth between the kitchen and the dining room. Ulysses and Frigga tried to persuade them to sit and eat with their guests, but Anne shook her head and went back for another platter.

"She is just like Martha," whispered Harold to Susan. "I read about her yesterday in Luke 10."

Susan nodded and smiled. She was very happy, very hungry and very curious. She was also a slow eater. Halfway through her roast beef and glazed carrots, but long before the huckleberry pie, she noticed that Ulysses had finished and was waiting for desert. "Ulysses, will you please tell us why Loki was trying to kill the Grandmother and where Hagen fits into the picture?"

Ulysses leaned back in his chair and stretched out his long legs before he spoke. "Until last night I was not sure myself, but Hagen has finally confessed to his crimes, and I have received a full report from one of the elders on the Ruling Council of Earth-Two.

"As you know the Ruling Council has worked very hard at keeping our two worlds separate. They have always believed that God Himself would bring them together at the proper time. Earth-One has invented machines that fly, machines that travel underwater and many other wonderful things, but the Mother Tongue is not known there. Earth-Two has kept alive the knowledge of the Mother Tongue, but life here is still somewhat primitive.

"Ten years ago one of the elders of the Council was murdered, and a new man was chosen to fill his place. A few years after that another murder took place and then another. Security for the Ruling Council was increased, and no more elders have been killed, but the three new members have been trying to turn the Council to their own ends. Their goal was to persuade the Council to mount a secret invasion of Earth-One and to bring its major leaders under their power.

"They worked in secret by threatening the families of our elders. Usually they killed one member of the family and then threatened to kill more if the elder did not vote with them. The elders never knew where the threats were coming from because messages always arrived in sealed envelopes that showed up mysteriously in their rooms. The elders were warned not to talk to each other, so none of them knew how many others had been threatened.

"Loki was their assassin, but the evil elders never dealt with him in person. They always found some willing accomplice to contact him. That is where Hagen came in. When I brought Hagen's band of rebels in for trial, one of the evil elders went hunting for him. He guessed that since I could not find Hagen's body, he might have escaped the landslide. He located Hagen while I was busy with the trial and easily persuaded him to join in their plot. Then he taught Hagen how to use mind-talk and gave him a crash course in English.

"Hagen found Loki, and the two men came here, but not together lest they arouse too many suspicions. The Grandmother's second son is a member of the Ruling Council, and Loki's task was to kill her just before a crucial vote sometime this summer. Hagen was supposed to stay in the village, but on his way through San Francisco, he had met a man who was engaged in buying and selling children. Hagen figured he did not need to be in the village to relay the elder's instructions to Loki, so he bought the sailboat and hired two men to take him back to San Francisco where he began rounding up stray boys and girls. Everything would have gone according to plan if you children had not showed up to rescue his captives.

"When Frigga and I captured Hagen, the plans of the evil elders began to unravel. They were afraid that Hagen might expose them to save his own life, so they made sure he was protected and treated well. Since Hagen never became very good at mind-talk, it was hard for him to make contact with Loki. Their conversations were short and infrequent, otherwise Hagen might have learned sooner that three children from Earth-One were in the village. The incident at the old tourmaline mine made Loki suspicious. He knew then that you had extraordinary abilities, and he decided to report you to Hagen. Hagen realized that the whole operation was in jeopardy, so he ordered Loki to kill the Grandmother and you three children, and then to get out of town. If Frigga and I had arrived five minutes later, he would have succeeded. I thank God for bringing both of us here at the same time. Loki might have defeated either one of us alone."

Harold, Susan, and William sat quietly for a few moments, thinking about how close they had come to death. It had never occurred to them that anyone might be stronger and more skillful in the Mother Tongue than Ulysses. Finally William spoke.

"Did you know, Grandmother, what Loki planned to do? Why did you leave the village? Why did you refuse to answer me out there beside the stream? Why didn't you even turn around to face Loki? Surely you must have known he was right behind you."

The Grandmother smiled as she reached across the table to rumple the boy's hair. "O William, have you ever in your life asked just one question at a time?" She paused for a moment before continuing. "I am one of the few people left in Earth-Two who knew Loki when he was a ranger—the head of rangers, actually. That was before he went bad and became a professional assassin. When he came to my village, I assumed he had come to kill me as he had already hunted down and murdered others who could identify him. I gave no sign that I recognized him, but later that day I contacted my son—the one who is a member of the Ruling Council. He had not yet been threatened, but he suspected that some members of the Council had been. My son wanted to send help, but he did not know whom he could trust. If there was a conspiracy, he did not know who might already be a part of it. He almost spoke to Ulysses, but fear held him back.

"I cannot explain it, but during the past week my heart has become heavy with the certainty that Loki would act soon. I went out into the forest last night sure that he would follow and sure that I would die. I wanted to meet him alone so that you and others in the village would not be hurt. When William called out to me from the edge of the meadow, I hesitated to turn around. If my eye had only flickered in your direction, I knew that Loki would notice and discover you. I did not expect him to take the coward's way out, though. I am sure he threw the stone in order to knock me senseless before he finished me off. He has killed so many brave men in face to face combat—what did he have to fear from an old lady?"

The Grandmother's voice dropped to a husky whisper and a tear glistened in the corner of her eye as she continued. "I wonder why he turned away from the right. He could have been as great a ranger as Ulysses, perhaps the greatest of all time. Harold, Susan, William, never forget what Loki might have been. God has given you wonderful abilities, and the Evil One will do all he can to turn you away from the Lord Jesus Christ. He may try to make you bitter toward God. He may try to enlist you in some terrible cause that seems noble. He may try to make you proud and self-confident. I have come to love you this summer, and if God spares me for a few more years, I want see what God has planned for you."

After the Grandmother finished speaking, Anne asked her husband to serve the huckleberry pie while she poured out eight cups of hot mint tea. The tea was welcome because an unseasonable rain had fallen during the night, and the day was cool. During dessert the conversation turned to other topics— what Frigga had seen in villages to the north, where Ulysses planned to go next, and when the children were going home.

"I miss Dad and Mom, and my own bed" said William, "but I also want to stay here as long as possible so I can continue my lessons with the Grandmother."

"We will leave in a week," answered Ulysses. "P. C. will take us back to San Francisco. His ship sustained some damage from a recent storm, so his crew needs to make repairs. They also need to replenish their supplies of food and water."

To Susan, the week seemed hardly to have begun before it was over. She did not see much of William, who spent most of his time with the Grandmother, but she and Harold had to tell their story over and over again to curious visitors from neighboring villages and farms. The day before they left, the village held a festival to honor the children and the rangers who had rescued their beloved Grandmother. In the morning there were races and games for the children. In the afternoon the men competed at archery and wrestling. For supper the village roasted three large pigs in earth-covered pits. Farmers brought in ears of the first-ripe corn, and the ladies baked their favorite pies and cakes. There was no zucchini or broccoli or asparagus, for which Harold and Susan were very thankful. (Only William was disappointed.)

As the sun went down, outsiders began collecting their children and their things and heading for home. Many of the villagers drifted over to the inn, and Susan found herself alone for the first time in a week. Quietly she slipped away and walked down to a large rock near the river where she could sit and watch the stars come twinkling into view. Arcturus and the summer triangle—Vega, Altair and Deneb—appeared first, followed by lesser diamonds of the sky. It was a perfect evening, clear and warm, but not sticky.

"Miss, Susan, "may I join you?" A year ago she might have been surprised by the voice behind her, but her ranger-trained senses had made her aware that someone was coming.

"Yes, Pete. There have been so many people around this past week that I haven't had time to say a proper farewell to you or to Al. Come, sit here beside me."

The tall man settled down beside the girl, and for a few minutes neither of them spoke. It was a comfortable silence between friends, a silence that Susan was reluctant to break. Finally Pete said, "Miss Susan, we have been through quite a bit together during these past few months. You, Harold, William, and now the Grandmother have turned all of my ideas about life upside down."

"What do you mean, Pete?"

"I used to think that if I didn't help myself, no one else would. I took whatever I could get, whenever I could get it. I didn't consider the feelings or needs of anyone besides myself. Then I met you and the others. You are different. You live to serve. You risked your lives to save the kidnapped children, and when you rushed down to face Loki, you could easily have been killed."

"We did not do more than you and Al tried to do," answered Susan. "Almost last thing I saw was you lying unconscious in the meadow where Loki had tossed you."

Pete's answer came slowly as if he were choking on the words. "I might not have done anything at all if Al had not grabbed my hand and started running. Miss Susan, I love you—and the boys, too—but I might have stood still and watched you die." Pete put his face down into his hands and began to weep. For several minutes Susan sat beside him, rubbing his back with her hand as he shook with uncontrollable sobs.

When he was quiet again, Susan said softly, "Jesus is the one who makes us different. He lived to serve others, and He died to save everyone who trusts in Him. We are not just trying to follow His example. It is more than that. When Jesus rose up from the grave and went into heaven, He sent His Holy Spirit to give us new life. The Spirit of Jesus has come to live in us—in Harold, and in William, and in me. The apostle Paul explained it this way: 'I have been crucified with Christ; and it is no longer I who live, but Christ lives in me; and the life which I now live in the flesh I live by faith in the Son of God, who loved me and gave Himself up for me' (Galatians 2:20).

"Pete, if you receive Jesus as your Savior, He will forgive you for all of your sins, including your selfishness. He will come to live in you. He will give you a new heart and make you a new man. Is that what you want?"

"Yes, Miss Susan. That is exactly what I want."

So the man and the girl held hands and bowed their heads as he opened his heart to the Savior. After they had prayed, Susan turned to look up at the stars again. She had been taught that when someone received Christ, he should be helped to find assurance of salvation. Somehow that seemed like the wrong approach for Pete, so she remained quiet. Pete followed her gaze into the heavens, and for half an hour they said nothing. Several meteors flashed across the sky. "Probably the Perseids," thought Susan, and still they did not speak.

By an unvoiced, mutual consent they rose together and walked slowly up the path toward the village. "I think Jesus really has come in," said Pete. "I feel much lighter, as if someone has taken a heavy load from my back."

Susan smiled and squeezed his hand. Suddenly her summer

was complete, and she felt in her heart that it was time to go home.

ABOUT THE AUTHOR

John K. LaShell has a BA from Moody Bible Institute, an MA from Talbot Theological Seminary in LaMirada, California, and a PhD from Westminster Seminary in Philadelphia. He has served churches in Wisconsin, Montana, and Pennsylvania. For seven years, he taught humanities as an adjunct professor at a branch campus of Penn State. He has been the pastor of Grace Community Church in Allentown, Pennsylvania, for the past 20 years.

His wife and helpmeet, Heather, is a Registered Nurse. They have two children and four grandchildren. Heather and John ("Hither and Yon") enjoy walking, canoeing, and traveling together.

Dr. LaShell is the author of two previous books:

The Beauty of God for a Broken World: Reflections on the Goodness of the God of the Bible, (CLCPublications, 2010).

Limping Christians: Help for Those Who Hobble along the Path of Life (self-published, 2014).

Information about his books, audio sermons, contact information, and a few other tidbits may be found at **www.Godisbeautiful.com**. Outlines of other books in preparation may be found on the website as well.

17663876R00142

Made in the USA
Middletown, DE
03 February 2015